The new Zebra Regency Romance logo that you see on the cover is a photograph of an actual regency "tuzzy-muzzy." The fashionable regency lady often wore a tuzzy-muzzy tied with a satin or velvet riband around her wrist to carry a fragrant nosegay. Usually made of gold or silver, tuzzy-muzzies varied in design from the elegantly simple to the exquisitely ornate. The Zebra Regency Romance tuzzy-muzzy is made of alabaster with a silver filigree edging.

MASQUERADE

Celeste smiled as his gaze lingered on her costume.

"I was hoping you might dance for me."

"Do you mean *with* me?"

"No. I hoped I could persuade you to dance *for* me, as Salomé once danced for Herod."

When he reached out to her, she held her breath, transfixed by his nearness. Lifting the end of one of her filmy veils, he said, "Dance for me. For me alone."

Trying to break the spell, she stepped back, forcing her gaze from his. But he eased his fingers under her veil, caressing the side of her face, sending tingling shocks through her. As her pulses raced, her mouth opened slightly and she felt the tip of his forefinger on her tongue. Impulsively, she kissed his finger. Horrified by what she'd done, Celeste gasped and drew back. She felt the veil pull away, baring her shoulders. Suddenly, his arms encircled her waist and he drew her toward him, pressing her body to his. Then his lips [illegible]

"Salomé," he br[illegible] ers. "Salomé . . ."

An Improper Alliance

Olivia Sumner

ZEBRA BOOKS
KENSINGTON PUBLISHING CORP.

ZEBRA BOOKS

are published by

Kensington Publishing Corp.
475 Park Avenue South
New York, NY 10016

First printing: December 1992

Printed in the United States of America

Chapter 1

Celeste Prescott, attractive, rich, possessing a happy disposition and gifted with enough cleverness to avoid making men overly aware of that cleverness, seemed to have all the attributes necessary to assure a steady stream of proposals of marriage.

Her friends in Guildford, where she attended Miss Yardley's School for Young Ladies, knew better. As did her acquaintances in Southampton, where she had been born and was subsequently raised by her guardians, Mr. and Mrs. Sebastian Morhouse, following the untimely deaths of both her parents. These friends and these acquaintances, in fact, would have evinced amazement on hearing that Celeste had received even a single such proposal. As it turned out, the eligible gentlemen of both Guildford and Southampton gave them no reason to be surprised.

There was one exception to this generally held opinion; that naysayer was M. Gerard DuChamp, the seventy-year-old music master at Miss Yardley's School, an emigré who had fled France during the

Revolution almost thirty years before. M. DuChamp taught Celeste the intricacies of the pianoforte and, though her playing could only be called undisciplined, he detected an ardor to her performances that caused him to fondly recall various amorous adventures in Paris during his not altogether chaste youth.

When Celeste reached the age of twenty-one on the twenty-seventh of December, 1816, at which time by the terms of her father's will she was to receive a considerable inheritance, she discovered to her astonishment and dismay that she was, in fact, penniless. Mr. Morhouse, acting unwisely if not illegally, had misused the bulk of the Prescott fortune to enter into a series of speculative investments in merchant ships which possessed a penchant for suffering the double misfortune of foundering in foreign waters while being underinsured.

The legality or illegality of Mr. Morhouse's squandering of the Prescott funds was never established by a court of law as shortly before the losses were revealed to the light of day, he and his wife precipitously departed not only Southampton but England as well. They intended, it was generally supposed, to employ the little that remained of the Prescott monies to recoup their losses in an atmosphere of greater freedom from the interference of courts or insurance companies. There were those who claimed they had set sail for Australia, others said Brazil, while still others thought the United States of America was to be their final destination.

And so Celeste, bewildered by this sudden dashing of her expectations, was set adrift in an indifferent world at the start of her twenty-second year with prospects little better than those of one of the ill-fated Morhouse sailing vessels.

Since she had been educated to be a gentlewoman, she found herself with few skills of any value whatever. She sewed, she knitted, her handwriting was considered exceptional and, as a result of M. DuChamp's instruction, she played the pianoforte passably well. She shunned whist and other card games but she excelled at solving riddles and conundrums. On the debit side of the ledger of her talents was her singing—off-key, and her artistic attempts, which had been dismissed as worse than hopeless by a succession of drawing masters.

Because she enjoyed the company of children and they liked her in return, she seemed destined to seek employment as a governess and, if successful, to remain one for the remainder of her life. While this prospect did not perturb her overmuch, neither did she look forward to such a career with enthusiasm.

At this crucial moment, faced with the realization she must come to a decision as to her future without delay and yet reluctant to take the first step along a path seeming to offer no chance for a change of heart, a letter arrived from her cousin, Lola Argent.

Miss Argent, a spinster of a certain age, had lived in London all her life. Because Celeste, being tall with light brown hair and a fair complexion, resembled her mother, who had been Miss Argent's favorite aunt, she offered her suddenly destitute cousin a temporary home—her letter explained that her nerves could not tolerate a prolonged stay—during which Celeste would be free to explore her limited alternatives in town. In a postscript she mentioned having heard that a Mrs. Jane Gordon was seeking a gentlewoman to be a companion to her daughter during the months of February, March and April.

Not only did Celeste have little to keep her in Southampton, in the course of infrequent visits to her cousin she had been enthralled by the bustling excitement of London. Still another attraction was the possible position with Mrs. Gordon; its short duration would allow her time to consider alternatives.

She replied by return mail, accepting her cousin's kind offer.

"Lord-a-mercy," Miss Argent exclaimed when Celeste arrived the following week, "all the way from Southampton by mail-coach? A young lady traveling alone? I'm flabbergasted."

"I must become accustomed to being on my own," Celeste told her.

"And to think," Miss Argent said, "I spend half a day convincing myself it's safe to venture out of this house for the five minute walk to Bond Street." She lowered her voice. "You must understand, my dear, I discovered early in life that I had the misfortune to inherit the Argent nerves."

Celeste soon guided the conversation away from the curse of the Argent nerves to Mrs. Jane Gordon.

"Agnes told me," Miss Argent said. "Did she perhaps hear it from Becky, the Davis's nanny? They always know more than we do, don't they? By they, I have reference to the servants. I have no acquaintance with the lady myself. By the lady I refer to Mrs. Gordon."

"Do you know how old her daughter is?"

Miss Argent shook her head. "Did Agnes say the mother's a widow? Yes, I'm certain she did. When I expressed interest, thinking at once of you, my dear Celeste, Agnes became a clam. That girl can be so infuriating! Yet she meant to spare me worry, I expect, since she does have my best interests at heart. Might the Gordon child be afflicted in some way, poor dear thing? Agnes would be loath to tell me, of course, knowing how distressed I become when forced to dwell on the suffering of others."

Since Miss Argent had obtained Mrs. Gordon's address, Celeste wrote at once expressing interest in the position and listing her qualifications. A week passed with no reply, during which time, despite Celeste's cheerful attentions, Miss Argent's nerves frayed at an alarming rate. At last Mrs. Gordon replied, inviting Celeste to call at her home just off Grosvenor Square at four on the following Thursday afternoon.

At ten minutes before the appointed time, beneath a lowering January sky, Celeste paused on the flagstone walk to look up at the quietly dignified Gordon townhouse. A tremor passed through her, a shiver both of apprehension—because she faced the unknown—and of excitement since she sensed she stood at the threshold of an adventure that could quite possibly change her life.

When she had questioned Agnes about Mrs. Gordon, the maid had professed ignorance. While Miss Argent suspected Agnes was concealing something, this belief could perhaps be a figment of her aunt's active and doleful imagination. Whether or not she now faced more than met the eye, Celeste, who had never before been a supplicant, had no notion of how best to present herself to her prospective employer. Her uneasiness was compounded by having learned that positions for which she was qualified were in short supply.

Drawing in a deep breath, she climbed the steps and rang the bell. She was ushered into the drawing room, an ornate chamber of gilt and ivory, and was surprised to find the draperies closed and the room lit by candles and the blazing fire. Her attention was immediately drawn to the portrait of General Percival Gordon above the fireplace. The general, an imposing craggy-faced warrior with a surfeit of medals displayed on his chest, held an unsheathed sword in one hand while his other rested on the North polar regions of a globe on which England and her possessions were colored a vibrant red. The general, she thought, must have been Mrs. Gordon's late husband.

"The general had two great disappointments in life," said a voice from behind her.

Startled, Celeste turned to find a tall, dark-haired woman watching her from the doorway. In the soft light she appeared little older than Celeste, although her commanding bearing, her fashionably-cut carmine gown and her jewels lent her a regal air. In comparison, Celeste's white muslin seemed positively dowdy.

Preceded into the room by the scent of lilies-of-the-valley, the woman swept across to Celeste, clasping her hands in her own. "Miss Prescott," she murmured, "I'm Jane Gordon."

Standing beside Celeste, she looked up at the portrait. "One of his disappointments was being posted to Canada to serve under General Burgoyne to suppress the rebellion of the American colonies. The general always maintained that Gentleman Johnny should have pursued his career of writing for the theater rather than trying to make his mark on the battlefield."

Celeste's brow furrowed. Since that war had been all of forty years ago, Mrs. Gordon had to be much older than she appeared; even so, her marriage must truly have been of the May-December variety.

"His other disappointment was never siring a son and heir. I was but one in a long line of failed attempts."

Now utterly confused, Celeste asked, "The general wasn't your husband?"

"No, no, no, no. My father. When my dear Mr. Richmond passed away, I recaptured my maiden name."

Celeste considered this a strange way to describe an equally unusual course of action, but she said nothing.

Mrs. Gordon waved Celeste to a lyre-backed chair near the pianoforte, then sat on a sofa facing her. On closer scrutiny, her hostess appeared many years older than Celeste had thought at first, her seemingly youthful glow owing a great deal to the soft candlelight and still more to the liberal application of creams and powders. Though disapproving of artifice, Celeste had to admit that even without embellishment Jane Gordon would be a strikingly handsome woman.

"You may have deemed me dilatory in answering your letter," Mrs. Gordon said, "but I have a close friend who in turn has friends in Southampton, so I took the liberty of asking him to make a few discreet inquiries. Your references proved to be every bit as satisfactory as I may have wished."

Celeste waited hopefully.

"You didn't consider remaining in Southampton after your guardian left for parts unknown?" Mrs. Gordon asked.

Since it still distressed her to discuss the Morhouses, Celeste avoided mentioning them. "Most of my life has been spent at a school in Guildford, so I have few ties in Southampton." *Or anywhere else,* she added to herself.

Mrs. Gordon nodded. "Let me explain what I require. I love to travel and when I do I leave my daughter Rowena here in London, an arrangement eminently satisfactory to both of us. After I received an invitation to visit friends in Brighton next month, my sister agreed to stay with Rowena during my absence, but unfortunately Julia's delicate condition now precludes her leaving home."

"I understand you'll be away for two or three months."

"Yes, at least for February and March. During that time, Rowena requires a companion. She's such a sweet and amiable child, but rather flighty." Mrs. Gordon frowned. "Let me be completely truthful with you, Miss Prescott; you'll find me to be a great believer in candor. While I'm away I need to have someone here to make certain Rowena doesn't run off with the prince."

Celeste stared in astonishment. "Run off? With the prince?" She recalled one of Miss Argent's favorite words—flabbergasted. Now it was her turn to be flabbergasted. "How old is Rowena?"

"Almost nineteen." Mrs. Gordon smiled. "I can tell from your agape expression you expected my daughter to be much younger. No, no, no, no. Rowena's quite the young lady, pretty, charming, genteelly raised and most amiable. And yet she possesses a flaw. Don't we all?"

Celeste realized the question was rhetorical with no answer expected.

"My own weakness," Mrs. Gordon went on, "is always considering the good of others before thinking of myself. Which is why I want to be assured that my daughter has a suitable companion while I visit Brighton. Rowena's flaw is managing to see the good in everyone; she possesses little discrimination, especially where members of the opposite sex are concerned."

Celeste knew she should remain silent but couldn't help saying, "But surely you, Mrs. Gordon, could prevent her from marrying by refusing your consent."

"Did I mention marriage as my greatest fear? I think not." Mrs. Gordon paused to allow time for her meaning to become clear. "Rowena reminds me of myself in many ways," she said. "When I was her age—and that wasn't so many years ago, after all—I know how I would have responded if my mother had forbidden me anything. I would have wanted it all the more, perhaps disobeying her merely to be perverse. Isn't that the way all children are?"

Celeste didn't agree in the slightest. Some children might be perverse, she thought, but most were not. She, for one, had never been. Since she couldn't say yes, she said nothing.

"So if I actively oppose Rowena's folly," Mrs. Gordon said, "or if I bundle her off to Bath or some such place, she might very well behave foolishly by decamping with the prince for Gretna Green. Or Paris. Or doing something infinitely worse."

Celeste had difficulty imagining an evil prince; to her, all princes were charming, handsome and heroic. Their role in life was to rescue maidens, not to deceive them. "Is the gentleman really a prince?" she asked.

"Oh, yes, there can be no question of that. I had the young man thoroughly investigated and discovered he's everything he claims to be. Of course he's not a prince as we think of them, he's not an English prince, he comes from some obscure German kingdom with the unlikely name of Marien-Holstein."

"That's on the North Sea, isn't it?"

Mrs. Gordon fluttered her hand vaguely. "The kingdom lies somewhere east of here in the direction of Russia. Or Finland. Pray don't misunderstand me, I have nothing against princes. In fact I once knew an Italian, not a prince, of course, but Louis Nannini was a count, the eldest son of a noble Tuscan family . . ." Her voice trailed off. "It's not the generality of princes I find objectionable, it's this particular prince."

"His character leaves a great deal to be desired?" Celeste prompted.

"Precisely. He exhibits a plethora of vices, drinking to excess, imprudent gambling and a liking for women of ill repute to name but a few of the more obvious. Not that many men of the *ton* don't have similar failings, they do. I recall my friend Lord Blankenship—" She stopped abruptly. "Prince Lothar, however, carries his failings to inexcusable depths. Lothar. His very name predisposes one to dislike him."

"He certainly sounds unsuitable."

"Unsuitable? Nay, the prince is utterly impossible. I have yet to tell you the worst. While he pays court to my daughter, the prince is betrothed to another."

Shocked, Celeste stared at Mrs. Gordon. "And your daughter still professes a partiality for him?"

"I understand your incredulity. Alas, she doesn't seem to realize the enormity of her indiscretion."

Celeste began to be assailed by second thoughts. Should she become a companion to such an imprudent young lady? Was she putting herself in a position where she would be forced to become involved in an unsavory intrigue?

"The other young woman isn't English," Mrs. Gordon added. "She's Bavarian. I believe she makes her home in Munich or Stuttgart or some other such German place."

"I find it difficult to imagine a young lady allowing herself to lose her heart to such a monstrously wicked man."

Mrs. Gordon smiled faintly as though in reminiscence. "At times a woman's heart has reasons no one else understands, Miss Prescott. I hope you won't misunderstand me: Rowena has had extremely acceptable suitors. A year ago, to give you but one example, Mr. Hugh B. Garson offered for her and Mr. Garson, if you didn't know, is both amiable and wealthy. Alas, Rowena refused him despite all of my protests. She seemed to hold his liking for animals against him."

"How strange."

Mrs. Gordon shook her head. "I do sympathize with your unease. However, I need the help of someone like yourself, Celeste. May I call you Celeste? You come to me recommended as a young lady of high moral standards and unflinching honesty."

The compliment brought a flush to Celeste's cheeks. "I have always attempted to obey the ten commandments."

"As do we all."

"There are those who believe I tend to be too truthful."

"Living in society at times requires a white lie or two, and perhaps a bit of dissembling here and there."

Feeling as strongly as she did on this point made Celeste speak up. "I disagree. Occasional small mistruths lead to frequent large mistruths and soon one is enmeshed in a web of deceit and duplicity."

Mrs. Gordon raised her eyebrows and then nodded as though something that had been puzzling her had at last become clear. "I wonder if the *ton* is prepared for a completely truthful young lady."

"I don't believe in cutting my cloth to fit the fashion of the moment."

"Thus dooming yourself to be always out of style.

Be that as it may, I fear we digress. I don't demand miracles from you, Celeste, only watchfulness. Besides, I assure you I possess more than one string to my bow. Though I have other plans to thwart Rowena's entanglement, I must rely mainly on the young lady who will be my daughter's companion." Mrs. Gordon leaned forward, extending a hand toward Celeste. "I require your help; my daughter needs you even though she might not realize it. Will you help me by helping Rowena?"

How could she refuse such a heartfelt appeal? "I will," Celeste promised.

"Good." Mrs. Gordon rose. "May I expect you on Monday next?" When Celeste nodded, she said, "Excellent. My daughter will be here and, that very evening, you'll meet the prince at the Haverford's dinner party."

Minutes later Celeste was once more standing on the walk, dazed by the sudden conclusion of the interview, surprised that she had been offered the position and even more surprised she had accepted that offer. It had never occurred to her she might one day be the paid companion to a gentlewoman's wayward daughter.

She drew in a deep breath of the sharp winter air. No matter what lay ahead, she silently vowed, she'd do all in her power to protect Rowena Gordon from the attentions of this reprehensible prince.

Chapter 2

". . . and so, my dear mother, after a long and tedious journey I have arrived in Marien-Holstein and taken up residence for a few days at the Halbinsel Hotel before traveling on to visit Herr Golze and his family." Roderic paused in his writing as he recalled how much he had once enjoyed travel. Now he considered it a tedious and uncomfortable bore.

"I find the service and the accommodations at the Hotel excellent, as always," he wrote, "and the only item I could possibly complain of—and I have not gone to the trouble of doing so since it is so insignificant—is the poor quality of the soap."

Hearing a tapping on the door to his room, Roderic Courtney-Trench, Earl of Campion, again paused, and with an impatient glance over his shoulder, called, "Come in."

The door opened and Giselle, the hotelkeeper's pert fair-haired daughter, smiled at him as she curtsied. "I am here to prepare your bed," she told him in German.

Making a pretense of indifference, Roderic waved his hand toward the mound of blankets. "Whenever you please." His German, though accented, was nevertheless fluent.

He returned to his letter but to his surprise found himself unable to call to mind any other details of his wearying journey from Paris to Marien-Holstein. Glancing behind him, the last of his interest in writing vanished when he saw Giselle leaning over the bed; the low decolletage of her peasant blouse offered an enticing glimpse of the curves of her breasts.

Roderic had been told by several self-proclaimed authorities that Giselle was unapproachable. And yet there had been an indefinable something in the way she had looked at him the night before when she showed him to his room that made him wonder. And hadn't she, when he glanced at her just now, held his gaze a few seconds longer than necessary?

"Is there anything else you require, Lord Campion?" she asked as she finished plumping the pillows.

When he swung around in his chair to face her, the look in her blue eyes sent an anticipatory tingle along his spine. There must be some request he could make, he told himself, some way to give her an excuse to linger. While he enjoyed intrigue, the simplest approach often proved to be the most successful.

"The soap," he said. "I find the hotel's soap most unsatisfactory."

She glanced at the night stand where a thick yellow bar rested in a dish. "We have much better soap," she said. "White and soft, round and scented, just large enough to fit comfortably in a man's hand. Do you wish me to bring you some?"

"If you would."

As she walked to the door she looked back at him as though a difficulty had suddenly occurred to her. "Our best soap is stored on a high shelf," she said. "If, perhaps, Lord Campion, you could come with me to help?"

He smiled. "Of course, the pleasure will be mine." He'd been right about Giselle, he thought, congratulating himself. His instincts rarely failed where women were concerned.

"The soap is stored in a closet on our uppermost floor," she told him as he followed her along the hall.

At that moment a soldier wearing the distinctive crimson-plumed shako of the Palace Guard trotted up the stairs from the hotel lobby. "Lord Campion?" he asked.

Roderic nodded; the soldier bowed, reached inside his greatcoat and brought forth a sealed letter. When Roderic started to thrust the letter into his pocket the soldier shook his head. "My orders," he said, "require me to insist you read the message at once."

With a "what choice do I have?" shrug toward Giselle, Roderic broke the seal, unfolded the single sheet of paper and scanned the message.

"Damn," he said in evident surprise. "The king requests my immediate presence at the palace."

"I will escort you," the soldier told him.

"The king?" Disbelief threaded through Giselle's voice.

Roderic showed her the letter. "Signed by King

Harlan Reinhardt himself."

Giselle's eyes widened when she saw the royal signature. "When the king commands," she said, "one must obey."

He reached out and touched the side of her face with his fingertips. "I will soon return," he told her. "For what you promised—the soap."

After the tiresome routine of donning his winter garb, he followed the soldier from the hotel and then, his head bowed against the chill wind off the North Sea, across the cobbled square to the magnificent old palace.

At the entrance to the palace grounds, sentinels snapped to attention and the iron gates swung open. Roderic and his escort climbed a long flight of stone steps to an anteroom where he noticed an eager young man—he couldn't have been more than sixteen—waiting for an audience. Roderic frowned—something about the youth seemed familiar; he could have sworn he'd seen him before but couldn't recall where or when.

An officer dismissed Roderic's escort, then bowed him into still another chamber where a liveried servant took his coat, scarf, hat and gloves. The castle, Roderic couldn't help noting, was exceedingly drafty. Poor heating, he decided, wasn't confined to England.

He was ushered through another door into another anteroom; a final double door, guarded by two soldiers, opened and he saw, at the far side of an enormous room, the king seated behind a large baroque table in murmured conversation with his chamberlain. Beyond them two high narrow windows looked out over the white-capped sea.

"Lord Campion," Roderic's escort announced.

After nodding his chamberlain and the officer from the room, the king stood and walked around the table. Roderic gave a perfunctory bow. The king, young, dark and the proud possessor of a small moustache, strode to him. "My dear friend," he said, embracing him.

The intimacy of the greeting surprised Roderic. Though he'd been a friend of the king's nephew for a year during the time they were both at Oxford, he'd met the king only once and then but briefly.

"Your Highness," he said warily.

"And did you enjoy Paris?" the king asked.

"I found the first twenty-four hours stimulating, the following two days pleasant and the remainder of my visit a frightful bore."

"Speak English, please. I study English from Mr. Davies. A beastly difficult language, your English." With his arm around Roderic's shoulders, he led him to a chair near the crackling fire. "Near the fire it is devilishly hot," he said, "away from the fire it is devilishly cold."

"And who is Mr. Davies?" Roderic asked.

"A bang-up gentleman, a paragon, a top-of-the trees Corinthian who fled England to escape the dunning of the cent percenters."

"Ah, yes, the dastardly moneylenders."

"A professor at our university offered to teach me English," the King said. "I refused; I desire to learn the speech from a dab hand, not from a popinjay professor who has not a feather to fly with."

"A wise decision," Roderic said while doubting

the truth of his words. Recalling the young man in the antechamber, Roderic said, "Just before I entered, I saw a youngster I thought I recognized."

"By Jove, you must mean Hans Rugh. He saved the lives of his two sisters in a boating accident and so at noon I present him with the Legion of Merit."

"He's not English, then?"

"No, a citizen of our country."

Roderic frowned, certain that in time he'd remember who the young man called to mind. Since he sensed the king was not yet ready to reveal the reason for summoning him to the palace, he asked, "Does your kingdom still suffer from a dearth of daughters?"

"Dearth? I dare say I know not dearth."

"A lack. Not enough baby girls are born."

King Harlan shook his head sadly. "There are never sufficient; I do not like it above half. The royal family requires more birthings. If they are bits of muslin it would be a special blessing."

No, Roderic decided, learning English from Mr. Davies had not been an altogether wise decision. Though it was unlikely to do any harm.

"You look addled," the King said. "Is my English wide of the mark?"

"Not at all, I understand every word. My compliments to Mr. Davies, he must be an excellent instructor."

"By Jove, Mr. Davies is a nonesuch. I wish he could also teach the Reinhardts a method to create more delicate conditions among our spouses."

Roderic was aware that the prosperity, if not the very existence, of Marien-Holstein depended on a goodly supply of royal children. Over the centuries, these children, especially the amiable and attractive Reinhardt daughters, had married into the royal families of most of the kingdoms of Europe and then used their marital influence to assure the continued independence of the small kingdom.

In the last two decades, however, the goddess of fertility had deserted Marien-Holstein. Few children were born to the Reinhardts, causing consternation throughout the hundred square miles of the realm. The King himself had been married for more than five years and still his queen remained childless.

"I asked you to come to the palace today," the King told Roderic, "to chat, not as a king to a nonpareil visitor, but as one man to another. Marien-Holstein finds itself in a deuce of a coil. We are threatened on one border by the Germans, on the other by the Dutch and from the sea by the Russians. Since our defenses are not up to snuff we require help from the English."

"I have scant influence with my government."

"You do not understand. I need your help with my nephew, that ne'er-do-well Prince Lothar."

Did the young man in the anteroom remind him of Lothar? Roderic wondered. No, not Lothar, someone else.

"Mein Gott, his actions are a disgrace," the King said. As his voice rose in anger, the King had reverted to German. "We must sign a treaty with the English so their navy will protect us; in return we proposed to allow their fleet to make repairs at our harbor here in Marienhaven." He shook his head in exasperation. "Three months ago I dispatched my nephew to

London to negotiate a naval treaty. And what has he accomplished in all this time? Nothing."

"Lothar is young."

"Twenty-five is not young. When I was his age—" The king sighed. "I fear I misjudged the young man but now it's too late to send a replacement. I chose Lothar because he's been like a younger brother to me, he knows my thoughts and my plans better than I do myself. Besides, he is liked by all. In all the world he has but one enemy."

"And that enemy is?"

"The worst any man could have. Himself."

"Perhaps your majesty should travel to London."

The king shook his head. Lowering his voice, he confided, "I still hope to sire an heir. The queen cannot travel so I must remain here to perform my duties as a husband. For the good of the nation."

Duty could be tiresome, Roderic thought. He said, sympathetically, "I understand your predicament. As for Lothar, though, he seemed a capable enough young man when I knew him. I found him little different from the other students."

"Precisely. I've discovered that Lothar is like a mirror, a young man who reflects those who happen to be around him. When he is here with me in Marien-Holstein, there is no greater patriot. When he travels to your country, I'm told he immediately imitates the idle ways of the *ton,* indulging himself by sampling all of London's vices rather than paying heed to the business at hand."

As he began to perceive the king's reason for summoning him to the palace, Roderic frowned in consternation. Since he had no intention of foregoing his visit to the Golze's, he tried to think of ways to solve the King's problem. "Your majesty might send a trusted emissary to London to speak to Lothar," he suggested, "one who could impress on him the urgency of his mission, or else—"

The King held up his hand. "Only you, my dear Roderic, are in a position to help me. You were Lothar's best friend, a man he holds in the highest esteem. And he sees you as a kindred spirit since at Oxford you shared many of his—what shall I call them?"

How different I was then, Roderic thought ruefully. How I enjoyed being alive; not only for the gaming and drinking but for everything life had to offer. How hopeful I was, how idealistic, how naive, how happy. But none of that was any concern of the king.

"Might you say I shared his worldly enthusiasms?" suggested Roderic.

"The exact phrase I sought. You once shared his worldly enthusiasms although now, I am informed, you practice moderation."

"When a man approaches the age of thirty, he grows weary of many of the pleasures he once savored." Roderic smiled sadly. Imagine. To be world-weary at twenty-eight! "They all seem rather flat."

"That is one of the reasons I want you, Roderic, to be the next image Lothar reflects. No, don't shake your head, you underestimate your powers. Not only does Lothar hold you in the highest esteem, you have other traits that make you my ideal emissary. You are renowned for being sharp-witted, intelligent and clever. Your Rothschild coup, for example, is still the talk of all the financial centers of Europe."

"I claim little credit for that, since sending carrier pigeons to bring London the first word of Wellington's victory at Waterloo was Nathan Rothschild's inspiration, not mine. The Rothschilds were the ones who made huge profits by buying shares on the exchange as soon as they received the news."

"Yet you, Roderic, were clever enough to discover not only that they were buying but the reason behind their buying. And then you possessed the courage to follow their example."

Roderic shrugged. "I always prefer to place my wagers on winners, not losers. The Rothschilds have always been among the winners."

"Exactly the reason you were the one I asked to come here this morning. You, also, are a winner."

"Asked me to come here? Ordered might be a more accurate word."

The king wasn't entirely successful in suppressing his annoyance at being contradicted. "I request your assistance as a friend of Prince Lothar," he said stiffly, "not as a good friend of the kingdom of Marien-Holstein." He hesitated. "There is one additional difficulty I didn't mention. I fear a woman is involved."

"Women usually are involved in one way or another. And more often for ill rather than for good."

"Come now, Roderic, admit there are some women who appeal to the best in a man, to his natural courtesy, his spirit of generosity, his valor, his chivalry, his charity."

"Those women are few and far between. In fact, I don't recall ever having met one."

The King nodded. "True, they are rare and unfortunately the young lady I speak of is not one of them. Rather she encourages Lothar in his spendthrift ways, his slothfulness and his pursuit of pleasure."

"A prince is always in danger of being the object of the wiles of mercenary females. Though I am not a prince, more than a few of these women have set their caps and their traps for me."

"Lothar has the notion he's in love."

Roderic sighed. "Young men are always fancying themselves to be in love. What they love is the idea of love."

"I haven't yet told you the worst. While the young lady herself is merely unsuitable, her mother is impossible."

"The mothers of young ladies invariably remind me of protective dragons, constantly breathing fire."

"Perhaps this particular dragon is known to you. Her name is Mrs. Jane Gordon."

"I believe I know her by reputation. Is she attractive? Was she widowed while still young? Has she been under the protection of various gentlemen of the *ton* since her husband's death?"

"I see you do know her. She's notorious and, therefore, quite unacceptable. How Lothar allowed himself to become entangled with her daughter is a puzzle to me. He is, you realize, betrothed to marry the Princess Hildegarde."

"Surely the princess will provide a good excuse when the times comes for Lothar to disentangle himself from this Miss Gordon."

"He claims he has no such wish now and never will have. His infatuation with this adventuress is secondary, of course; having the naval treaty signed is my paramount goal. Will you travel to London as my emissary, Roderic? Will you help Marien-Holstein in its hour of need?"

He was tempted. Once, when he was younger and before he had learned to distrust everyone, including kings, he would have said yes without hesitation. But this wasn't his problem and he had no wish to involve himself in the tedious business of trying to solve it.

"I'm deeply sorry," he said. "There's nothing I can do."

"I refuse to beg you, Roderic." The king's voice was chill. "If you reconsider, let me know." The king stood; Roderic followed suit and bowed. The king nodded a curt dismissal.

As he passed through the antechamber, Roderic found the young hero standing in front of a large mirror nervously adjusting his cravat in preparation for his audience with the King. Glancing over his shoulder, he saw both of their faces reflected in the glass. The boy's eyes glittered with anticipation; his were lusterless. The boy's face was alight with hope; his stared back dully at him. And yet . . .

The hair rose on his nape. He knew now who the youngster reminded him of—no other than Roderic Courtney-Trench. A younger Roderic, an eager Roderic, a vital Roderic. A wave of sadness swept over him as he felt regret for all he had lost.

It's not too late, he told himself, perhaps I can be

that way again. He turned on his heel and walked swiftly back to the enormous room.

The king glanced up from the papers on his desk.

"When does the next ship leave for England?" Roderic asked.

"The *Narvik* sails within the hour. The next sailing after that is in three days' time."

"I'll leave today; I'll do all I can for Lothar," Roderic promised. "Will you have my luggage sent directly from the hotel to the *Narvik*?" The King nodded. "And will you notify Herr Golze?" Another nod.

All at once Roderic pictured the tempting Giselle leaning over his bed at the hotel.

"Have you forgotten something?" the King asked.

Roderic smiled slightly. "Only my soap," he said. "I was unhappy with the hotel's soap so I was promised a sample of another, reputedly vastly superior variety."

"They must have been referring to our Roemermann Soap. Herr Roemermann recently developed a new and secret formula to produce a soap much better even than your Pears. Unfortunately, you have no time now to receive your sample."

Roderic shrugged, raising his hands, palms up. "I probably would have soon tired of even the best of soap," he admitted, "and descended into the doldrums once again."

"You must make haste," the King said, embracing him. "Farewell. Thank you, my friend, and may God go with you."

As Roderic followed his escort from the palace, he vowed to do all in his power to help the king. Not only would he forcefully remind Lothar of his duty to his country, he would at the same time break the prince's ties to this predatory woman with the notorious mother.

He drew in a deep breath. By God, he felt more alive than he had in years.

Chapter 3

Early in the morning on the day before she was to begin her employment at the Gordon house, Celeste was surprised to receive the following letter from Mrs. Gordon:

My dear Miss Prescott,

Unexpected events in Brighton require my immediate presence in that city and so I find myself required to depart London sooner than expected. Will you consider me presumptuous if I impose upon your good nature by requesting that you to come to me as soon as possible?

Any sacrifice on your part will be greatly appreciated by one who considers herself to be more your friend than your employer,

Mrs. Jane Gordon

With no compelling reason to remain at Miss Argent's, Celeste hastened to complete her packing as soon as she finished breakfast and, following a farewell to her cousin, departed with no little trepidation for Grosvenor Square.

When she arrived with the trunk containing her belongings, she stood on the flagstone walk in front of the Gordon townhouse, looking about her at a scene of bustling activity. A traveling chaise waited in the roadway, the breath of the four horses sending white plumes into the cold January air. Several menservants, bent low by the heavy trunks they carried on their backs, staggered uncertainly down the steps to be met on the walk by others who struggled heroically to heave each piece of the seemingly unending avalanche of luggage up onto the roof of the chaise.

Just as Celeste decided to make her way up the steps, Mrs. Gordon appeared in the doorway, wearing a crimson traveling coat and a hat bedecked with ostrich feathers. Seeing Celeste, she gave a joyous cry and hurried down to her, preceded by the spicy scent of frangipani.

"My dear Celeste," she exclaimed, "how can I ever thank you enough for coming to me a day early? You are indeed a treasure." She gestured vaguely about her. "As you can see, you find me all in a dither for I must depart for Brighton within the hour. I fear our best laid plans are usually destined to become the playthings of fate."

How giddy Mrs. Gordon seemed, Celeste thought, how changed from the day of their first meeting. "If I could meet your daughter?" she suggested.

"Rowena. Yes, yes, certainly." Mrs. Gordon

turned and called, "Charles!" The burly coachman hurried to her, deferentially touching the brim of his hat.

"If you will have the goodness to see that Miss Prescott's trunk is taken to the green room," she told him. "The remainder of your luggage will arrive later?" she asked Celeste. "No? There is no more? Mercy, I never intended to commit a gaffe by suggesting you don't have a feather to fly with. I tend to say the wrong thing when I have to rush about like this."

She took Celeste's arm and propelled her up the steps. "You must make Rowena's acquaintance before I leave, of course you must, and my daughter is quite eager to make yours." When they entered the house, and after a servant had taken Celeste's coat, Mrs. Gordon said, "I chose the green room for you because of your quite remarkable emerald eyes. I admire them exceedingly."

Mrs. Gordon paused at the door to the drawing room and whispered, "Though Rowena is a sprightly, charming girl, you may find her just a wee bit spoiled. During my absence, I advise letting her have her own way except, of course, in anything that concerns that wretched prince."

Before Celeste could ask her to explain the precise meaning of these instructions, Mrs. Gordon bustled into the drawing room where a dark-haired young lady sat on a sofa with her back to them.

"Ah, darling Rowena," Mrs. Gordon said, "this is the companion I promised. I must tell you, Miss Prescott, Rowena has heard me sing your praises until she must be quite fatigued."

Able to think of nothing that would not prejudice Rowena against her, Celeste decided it was prudent to remain silent. In fact, she had no opportunity to speak since Mrs. Gordon plunged on. "Admit the truth, Rowena," she gushed, "have you ever set eyes on a more handsome young lady?"

Rowena, who had been reading a romantic novel, *Sense and Sensibility,* reluctantly laid her book aside and stood to face them. She was a pretty girl, Celeste thought, with black hair arranged in becoming ringlets, a pert face enlivened by a turned-up nose, and grey eyes. Her slender figure was accentuated by her morning dress of Mexican blue with a scalloped neckline and sweeping skirts trimmed with multiple rows of white braid.

"Mama," Rowena said after scrutinizing Celeste from her bonnet to her shoes, "I must admit she is every bit as handsome as you claimed." Her tone was much less enthusiastic than her words.

"Splendid! I was certain the two of you would become capital friends. And now I must bid you both *adieu.*" She embraced her daughter. "Promise to write me, Rowena." She darted a significant look at Celeste. "And you must write me as well," she said, "since I want to hear all the news from town."

As soon as her mother had swept from the room, Rowena glanced at Celeste, shaking her head. "I do love mama dearly," she said, "even when she embarrasses me almost to tears."

Not knowing what to reply, Celeste said nothing. She had expected Mrs. Gordon to be present during her first meeting with Rowena to smooth the way but instead she found herself completely on her own.

"How intolerable this must be for you," Rowena said, softening; "you must feel much as I did my very first year at Brighton when we went to the beach where I quite expected to be thrown into the deep water to sink or swim, though of course nothing of the sort occurred. This is so like mama to leave us to thrash about on our own."

"Your mother did seem to be in a hurry."

"Yes, a frightful hurry." Was there a touch of asperity in Rowena's voice? "And hurrying does make mama careless. Shall we sit by the fire? When I watch the flames dance I have the most romantic imaginings."

As soon as they were seated, Rowena said, "I must admit you look not in the least like I expected."

Celeste frowned. "I believe you told your mother quite the opposite."

"Mama is always happiest when I agree with her and so I make a practice of doing so whenever possible. The opposite? You, or so mama has been telling me, often do quite the opposite of what is expected."

Celeste thought she understood what Rowena had in mind. "Do you mean I try to be perverse? Not at all. I do attempt to tell the truth. Not only when the truth is convenient, but always."

"How unusual. Most people claim they always tell the truth, a claim that's an untruth in itself." Rowena smiled mischievously. "We really must have a testing," she said, frowning as she thought. "Did you like my mother's scent? The frangipani?"

"I find the scent pleasant when used in moderation. In my opinion, your mother uses it to excess."

"Mercy!" Rowena raised her eyebrows, then giggled. "Those are my sentiments exactly. I do believe you and I think alike." She glanced sideways at Celeste. "When I made the observation that your appearance surprised me, you neglected to ask what I expected you to be like. Have you no curiosity about it?"

"I always believe if someone wants me to know something that person will eventually tell me."

"We are *not* alike after all, since I have no patience with secrets and so I invariably ask. But I shall tell you nonetheless—I expected you to be either terribly dowdy or else I thought you might resemble mama in some way. Yet neither is the case, since I find you quite handsome, just as I truthfully told mama."

Celeste felt her face redden.

"However," Rowena said, "when I saw how attractive you were, quite another thought entered my head. Since I have no expectation of your ever asking me what that thought might have been, I intend to tell you without delay. I said to myself, 'Mama is behaving deviously, as she so often does. She intends to employ this young lady to be my companion with the hope that Lothar will find her outrageously attractive and begin to flirt with her, thus precipitating a grand *contretemps.*'"

Celeste was taken aback. "I very much doubt that was your mother's intention. It definitely isn't mine."

"Of course not! I just wanted you to know what ran through my head when I first set eyes on you. Not that I believed it to be true."

Celeste blinked, realizing she had been taking Rowena much too seriously. Rowena's conversation—chat, she decided, would be a much better description—was like a copy of her mother's in that they both were inclined to say the first thing to pop into their heads.

"In the novel I was reading," Rowena said with a nod in the direction of the book on the table, "the heroines are two sisters, one who obeys the commands of her heart and the other who follows the dictates of her head. The one who invariably uses good sense is almost always right but her sister is by far the more engaging. I suspect I must be akin to that sister for I follow my heart even when my mother and all the rest of the world is telling me how mistaken I am."

"I believe in being sensible rather than rash," Celeste said.

"How wonderful! You and I are exactly like the sisters in the story. And we will come to love one another just as they do, even though we tend to be complete opposites." Rowena paused and, suddenly serious, asked, "Did mama tell you about Prince Lothar?"

Celeste, by now becoming accustomed to Rowena's sudden changes of direction, admitted she had.

"Mama considers the prince quite unsuitable," Rowena said, imitating her mother's disapproving tone. She sighed, then smiled dreamily. "As you yourself will observe at tomorrow's dinner party, the prince is nothing of the sort. Never in my life have I met a handsomer, more chivalrous or thoroughly agreeable gentleman."

Celeste refused to let this glowing assessment pass unchallenged. "Your mother informed me the prince is betrothed to another. If that is the fact, she requires no other reason to object to him."

"And did she supply you with any of the details of this so-called betrothal? No, I suspected not. The supposed match was arranged years and years ago by Lothar's father and his uncle the king without Lothar's knowledge or consent, arranged solely to further the interests of the kingdom of Marien-Holstein and with no thought given to Lothar's wishes. Lothar has no more feeling of tenderness for this young lady than, I suspect, she possesses for him. In truth, they have never so much as once set eyes on each other."

Surprised, Celeste hesitated before replying. "No matter what the circumstances," she said finally, "a gentleman is either committed to another or he is not, and in this case it appears that Prince Lothar is."

"How stiff you are! How frightfully encumbered with good sense! Not that Lothar has no faults, I admit he does, he possesses a few common to most gentlemen of the *ton,* but time will serve to change him for the better. Time and the influence of one who loves him and has his best interests at heart."

She means herself, Celeste realized. Any woman, she thought, who married with the hope that she would reform her errant husband had to be the greatest optimist in the world. And one of the most foolish.

"Have you ever thought of marrying?" Rowena asked.

"Of course, just as most women have at one time or another, but I refuse to let the idea of marrying and having children preoccupy me. Someday I may meet a compatible man of amiable disposition, a man who will earn my respect for his high standards not only of principle but of practice. A clergyman perhaps."

"A clergyman!" Rowena frowned. "Alas, if only I counted a clergyman among my acquaintances, I would introduce him to you at once. Wait, let me think, there was Mr. J. Richard Trevor, he was the gentleman with the unfortunate lisp and he never would reveal his first name, but I understand he obtained a living in a parish ever so far away in a wild and uncivilized region of the Scottish Highlands. I could make inquiries, since someone in the *ton* must know of an eligible clergyman."

Celeste smiled at Rowena's sudden enthusiasm for matchmaking. "I believe if a woman is fated to meet her intended, she will—without the assistance of others."

"And *I* believe fate more often than not requires one or more helping hands." She shook her head. "I never heard anyone express a preference for a clergyman before." Her hand flew to her mouth. "Not that I find the notion completely extraordinary, not at all, since even a clergyman must marry, if we are to have the wives of clergymen to perform charitable works."

"And," Celeste said, "if parish good works allow the wife sufficient time, to supply the world with a quiverful of babies, the boys destined to become clergymen in their turn and the girls to marry other men of the cloth and so repeat the process."

Rowena glanced at her aslant, as though not quite certain whether Celeste spoke in all seriousness. "We may happen upon a clergyman at the masquerade," she said, "though I would be most surprised if we did. The masquerade! Did mama mention the masquerade?"

Celeste shook her head.

"The gala will be held in the ballrooms at Darlington House on Saturday a fortnight. Since I shall be attending, you will as well and so we must decide on your costume. As for myself, at first I intended to masquerade as a Spanish dancer, wearing a black mantilla, carrying castanets and with a single red rose in my hair. I may, however, change my mind." She put her hand to her chin. "As for you—?"

"Perhaps I should appear at the masquerade attired as a nun. Can you think of a better ploy to attract the attention of a man of the cloth in the unlikely event one should be present?"

"A nun wearing a habit? No, I do believe that might not be quite the—" Rowena stopped in mid-sentence. "You *are* funning me. A few moments ago I suspected you were, now I know it for a fact. The very idea, a nun at a masquerade!" She giggled. "Perhaps Harriette Wilson or one of her friends might appear so attired, but what can you expect from them?"

"Since I have no acquaintances in town who might recognize me, a simple mask should prove to be a sufficient disguise."

"No, no, no. Everyone is expected to appear in costume." She nodded vigorously. "I have an idea. Why not masquerade as someone completely at variance with your own true character? Perhaps a concubine from a Persian harem. Or an actress."

"Most certainly not."

Rowena smiled. "I was teasing you; after all, you were funning me and turnabout is fair play." She closed her eyes in thought. "I have another notion. At tomorrow's dinner you could appear in your most dowdy Southampton clothes and then at the masquerade come as a princess wearing a dazzling gown with jewels and a tiara. The contrast would quite overset everyone."

Celeste, not at all taken with any of Rowena's ideas, said, "Perhaps we should sleep on the choice of my costume."

"When we do decide, you must allow me to help you shop. The only thing I love more than clothes is to shop for clothes. Especially bonnets. Glaffney's, the milliners, is quite my favorite shop. Of course I enjoy shopping for most anything, not only gowns and bonnets. Did I tell you I intend to wear my white silk to the dinner party? I consider the gown my good luck talisman since I was wearing it last October on the night I met the prince at the Langley's ball."

Celeste frowned, wondering what she could wear to the dinner, realizing the gowns that had seemed quite the thing last year in Southampton were already hopelessly outmoded by London standards.

"I understand a friend of the prince will be with him at the dinner," Rowena said. "Lord Campion." Celeste was surprised to her the awe in her companion's voice.

"Should I know this Lord Campion?" The name meant absolutely nothing to her.

"I thought everyone did. At one time he was a boon companion of Lord Byron; he supposedly has repeatedly outmaneuvered everyone, including the Rothschilds, on the exchange; he fought a duel with Lord Livesay over the attentions he was paying to Livesay's wife; and he was scandalously involved with Lady Barthels and Ellen Courtney, the actress. And involved with both of those ladies at the very same time!"

"Your prince has dubious friends, to say the least."

"Dubious? I consider Lord Campion rather intriguing."

Celeste, taken aback, said nothing.

"Lothar and Campion were at Oxford together," Rowena said. "I never had the occasion to meet Lord Campion since he rather mysteriously left London four or five years ago and this visit is his first since. I know you must think me foolish, yet I find myself all agog at the very thought of meeting him."

"If he is suddenly smitten by you and so attempts to carry you off from the dinner party, I have no doubt your prince will fly to your rescue."

When Rowena, who was gazing into the fire, nodded and then sighed, Celeste decided her friend was imagining a daring midnight abduction followed by a wild pursuit on galloping horses along country roads culminating in a dramatic rescue. In a way she envied Rowena's impossibly romantic vision of life.

As for herself, she looked forward to meeting the prince. Would he turn out to be Mrs. Gordon's irredeemable scoundrel or Rowena's flawed yet gallant hero? On the other hand, her lips pursed in distaste at the very thought of his friend, Lord Campion. She abhorred his sort; she would certainly dislike him intensely.

She vowed to avoid him at all costs.

Chapter 4

Roderic and Lothar left the prince's townhouse arm in arm on a moonlit February night.

"To my club!" Lothar said.

"The hackney stand is on the corner."

"No, the walk is short. I love the chill of the winter air on my face, it invigorates me. And then to enter White's and be toasted first in the front and then in the back by one of their roaring fires. Wonderful!"

Roderic envied his friend's enthusiasm, his evident joy in being young and alive. "White's?" he asked. "You belong?"

"My dear Roderic, you yourself proposed me for membership in ought eight. Or was it ought nine? Don't you remember?"

Roderic shook his head. "Those times all run together in my mind to form a huge grayish blur. Byron's Dandy Club, Boodles, Brooks, White's. The gaming's devilishly deep at White's. Or was in my day."

"It remains so. And all the better, to my way of

thinking." Lothar lowered his voice though there was no one on St. James's Street near enough to overhear him. "I recently purchased, for a most modest sum, a method of wagering guaranteed to win at hazard."

"Oh my God." His voice showed his dismay.

"But Roderic, have you forgotten? You were once as full as a tick with methods for overcoming the gaming odds. I recall one for wagering on the horses at Tat's. And another for whist."

"You remember aright. However, have *you* forgotten how many of those schemes of mine were rewarded by success? If you have, let me refresh your memory. None. Not a solitary one. If White's learns you have a method for winning at their hazard tables, do you expect them to immediately bolt their doors against you? No, they will not, rather I expect they'll send a carriage to bring you to their gaming rooms, post haste."

Lothar shook his head sadly at his friend's lack of understanding. "My wagering method is based on the soundest of mathematical principles. For each of the past two days I've spent two hours in my rooms throwing the dice, making a long series of imaginary wagers and keeping a meticulous record of the totals. Upon my word, Roderic, the results are quite extraordinary."

Roderic feared that no words of caution would deter the prince from his reckless course, yet he felt obliged to try to reason with him. "What is this remarkable method?" he asked. "Could it be some variation of doubling your bet after a loss and proceeding to double until you win?"

"Certainly not!" Lothar cried in a mock-insulted tone. "Nothing so elementary. My method absolutely guarantees that I wager a greater sum when making a winning bet than I do on a loser. Be patient, Roderic, soon you'll see for yourself and be struck dumb with amazement. And wonder why the idea never occurred to you."

They crossed the street by weaving their way between the horses and iron-wheeled carriages clattering by on St. James, walked beneath the pair of glowing lamps in front of White's and entered the club. After they left their winter garments in the cloakroom, Lothar started toward the bar, nodding and otherwise responding to hearty greetings from all sides, but Roderic suggested they sit in the quieter Oak Room instead. Until now he and Lothar had only reminisced and talked in generalities; the time had come for a more serious discussion.

The older members of White's favored the Oak Room. As he and Lothar made their way to two overstuffed chairs near the fire, Roderic heard the rustle of newspapers interspersed with a few gentle snores.

When a waiter approached them, Lothar said, "Two rum fustians."

The waiter raised a doubtful eyebrow a quarter of an inch before inclining his head and departing.

Roderic experienced a stirring of pleasant memory. "Haven't had a rum fustian in years," he said.

"You were the one who taught me to appreciate the drink. Ages ago. I expect I can claim to be the only member of White's who still orders rum fustians even though they're quite the thing for this cold February night."

Roderic recalled that a rum fustian consisted of a concoction of beer, sherry, gin, the yolks of eggs, sugar and nutmeg, the ingredients stirred vigorously before being heated with a sizzling-hot loggerhead. The drink contained no rum whatsoever.

"Fustian rum—imitation rum," said Roderic.

How right and proper, he thought, that he had favored an imitation drink while leading what he now considered to be an imitation life. He had suspected then, and now heartily believed, that there must be something better for himself, more meaningful, yet he had failed to find it. And had almost given up the search before being challenged by King Harlan's appeal for help.

Roderic frowned as he watched Lothar dispatch his rum fustian with unwonted alacrity and proceed to immediately order a second. At least when *he* had visited the gaming tables he had made a practice of shunning intoxicants. Gambling was a serious endeavor requiring a man to have all of his wits about him.

"Gambling houses are always generous with spirits," he remarked. "They know from experience a gentleman in his cups is apt to take more than his share of foolish chances."

Lothar smiled, a bit smugly, Roderic thought. "The good Lord above blessed me with a limitless capacity for rum fustians," he said.

"I expect the drink must have become popular during a shortage of actual rum. Perhaps at a time the British Navy commandeered all of the supply."

This conversational gambit, intended to raise the matter of the hoped-for naval treaty, was a rather obvious ploy but represented the best Roderic could manage on the spur of the moment.

Lothar put down his empty mug. "You must have talked to my uncle about that treaty," he said.

Roderic had expected resentment but heard none in his friend's voice. "I did," he admitted. "He described the situation and requested my help."

"That damned admiralty of yours. I appealed to them, practically fell to my knees, did my best to move them to action and the result was less than nothing. The cruel fact is they don't give a damn about Marien-Holstein. If you English were still at war, mayhap someone would at least have the courtesy to listen to my plea. As it is—" He shrugged in hopeless frustration.

"If you have no objection, I intend to make inquiries," Roderic said. "Attempt to find someone with influence who owes me a favor or two."

"I wish you every success, though I expect you'll discover that whether Marien-Holstein continues to exist or vanishes from the map of Europe is of no concern to the English."

Though Roderic made no reply, he had to agree with his friend's gloomy assessment.

"We have no manufacturers," Lothar went on resignedly, "and in late years we have produced no young princesses to tempt the European royal heirs." He waved his mug to banish all further discussion of the naval treaty before finishing his fourth rum fustian. Standing, a mite unsteadily in Roderic's opinion, he rubbed his hands together in anticipation. "To the gaming rooms."

Roderic followed him along a hall and into a chamber redolent with cigar smoke. Walking past games of faro on his right and whist on his left, Lothar stopped in front of the first of the hazard tables. For several minutes they stood observing the play.

The gamblers placed their counters on the green baize table, the croupier shook the birdcage containing the three dice, the players murmured incantations to the goddess of chance, the croupier called the numbers showing on the dice: "Three, six, one," followed by the total: "Ten," the losing bets were raked away to add to the bank's large stacks and, finally, the winners were paid.

As he watched the ebb and flow of fortune at the table, Roderic felt a trace of his gambling fever return as he recalled the thrill of risking his all, of issuing a challenge to the fates and waiting expectantly for their immediate answer.

Lothar took a seat at the table, signed for a pile of counters and essayed a modest ten guinea bet on the "Even." The croupier shook and turned the birdcage, placing it on the table where all the players could see that the dice totaled twelve. An even number, paying even money. Lothar had won ten guineas.

At White's, a hazard player could wager on a number from one to six coming up on any of the three dice, or he could wager on the total of the three, on a total being odd or even, on a high or low total, or else on a raffle, a raffle being a triplet with each die showing the same number. On the rare occasions when a raffle was thrown only raffle bets were winners; all others lost.

Roderic placed an occasional small wager on the three sixes' raffle without success. Lothar, though, bet on every shake of the dice, always placing his money on the "Even," and soon amassed a sizable heap of counters. His strategy had become clear to Roderic almost at once: every time he lost he increased the size of his bet by ten guineas; every time he won he decreased it by the same amount.

"You never lose if you have the will to walk away when ahead," Roderic cautioned.

Lothar, obviously caught up in the excitement of the game and the headiness of winning, would have none of it. "White's owes me much more than this," he admitted, "and I intend to recoup every penny."

Slowly the run of even totals slackened and odd totals began occurring with alarming regularity. Increasing his bet with each loss, Lothar was soon wagering one hundred guineas, then, in what seemed a twinkling, two hundred on each cast of the dice. He paled, he seemed to shrivel in upon himself. Finally he leaned across the table and murmured a few words to the croupier who immediately made an unobtrusive motion with his hand.

At the signal, a shrewd-faced, fashionably dressed gentleman sauntered to the table. Roderic recognized him as George Raggett, the owner of White's, a man who, so it was whispered, always stayed at his place of business well after closing time to personally sweep the floor so he could pocket any counters lost by careless players. In all likelihood, Roderic thought, Raggett would end up wealthier than most of the habitués of his club, not so much from his floor sweeping as from the eight or more percent advantage the house enjoyed on every play.

Raggett glanced at Lothar, smiled and nodded his approval. As soon as Lothar signed another chit, the croupier piled more counters in front of him.

On the next cast of the dice three sixes appeared and Roderic received one hundred and eighty guineas in return for his one. Lothar's losses, however, continued to mount. Again the croupier summoned Raggett but this time the owner frowned and discreetly shook his head. Roderic could only admire Lothar's reaction—without a word of protest he sketched a bow and left the table.

"My method succeeded," Lothar insisted. "If only I had enough funds to pursue it to the end, I would have recouped all of my losses."

Roderic said nothing but wondered, as he suppressed a sigh, how many times he had heard similar plaintive "if onlys" from losers.

As they retrieved their greatcoats, Lothar was greeted effusively by a gentleman dressed in the first stare of fashion—he wore a black silk coat, a white waistcoat and an elaborately tied white cravat; a quizzing glass hung suspended from a gold chain around his neck and he gestured with a black cane topped by a gold knob.

Roderic, standing a short distance away, heard Lothar address him as Cecil.

"Some of us are on our way to Sophia's," Cecil said. As he leaned closer to Lothar and lowered his voice, his words became indistinguishable, but from his lascivious smile Roderic supposed he was detailing the various pleasures that awaited them.

At that moment a plan sprang fully formed into Roderic's mind. Since King Harlan had asked him to bring Lothar's courtship of the predatory Rowena Gordon to an end, what better way than to turn Lothar's weakness where women were concerned against him? Although Mrs. Gordon might abide the prince's drinking and gambling, she would certainly draw the line at public philandering.

Cecil, still smirking, started toward the door as he looked expectantly at Lothar. With no hesitation, the prince shook his head. Cecil raised his eyebrows in surprise but shrugged, said a few words, bowed stiffly—not necessarily because of the rebuff since his movements were constricted by his tight coat and high stiff collar—and walked off to join his carousing friends.

Lothar remained silent as he and Roderic once more made their way out onto St. James's Street. After a distant watchman proclaimed the time to be two in the morning, he said, "My uncle must have told you about Miss Rowena Gordon."

"I believe he mentioned her name," Roderic admitted.

"If only he could meet her he would be singing her praises instead of constantly castigating her. Not only is Rowena the most beautiful woman in all of London, she possesses every admirable female trait, including amiability, virtue, sensibility, vivacity and wit, to name but a few."

"A true paragon."

"I hear the skepticism in your voice, Roderic. Once

you meet her you, too, will fall under her spell. Ever since the day Rowena captured my heart, I've forsworn all other women."

Roderic groaned inwardly. Lothar claimed to shun the one vice that he, Roderic, could have used as a lever to separate him from Miss Rowena Gordon. Ah, well, he had other arrows in his quiver. Or would have as soon as he determined the exact lay of the land.

"Miss Gordon's mother," Roderic ventured as he began his reconnaissance, "is reputedly not above reproach."

"That may well be; in truth, 'tis well known by all except Rowena herself. However that may be, my good friend, it is the virtuous daughter I love, not her errant mother."

A black cat emerged from the shadows, crossed their path and ran into the shadows on the other side of the empty street.

"You, Lothar," Roderic said as he idly wondered if the cat was an omen signifying trouble ahead, "happen to be a prince of the kingdom of Marien-Holstein. You must be aware that a prince has many privileges but those privileges bring special obligations with them. A prince must be loyal to his family and to his country, he must place them above mere self interest. A prince marries not to satisfy himself, not for an ephemeral lust or even a supposed love, but to insure the happiness and prosperity of his subjects. Like it or not, Lothar, that is what being a prince entails."

"You sound exactly like an unholy combination of my father and uncle. Perhaps, since you were certainly preaching, I should say a holy combination."

"The fact is I agree with them." And, in his heart, he did.

Lothar nodded. "I understand why you came to London, Roderic. Though you may do your damnedest to disentangle me from this female, as my uncle would phrase it, I swear to you that nothing you might attempt will endanger our friendship. On the other hand, once you meet Rowena, who happens to be the sweetest, most charming girl in all the world, I expect you to become a convert to my cause rather than an opponent. Not you nor the king nor Mrs. Gordon will ever succeed in coming between Rowena and me."

"Mrs. Gordon?" Roderic, surprised to hear that Rowena's mother also opposed the match, stopped walking and looked at his friend.

"She tries to thwart us at every turn."

"I had supposed she favored you as a suitor." After all, he reminded himself, her reputation had rendered her daughter, if not damaged goods, certainly not completely saleable on the marriage mart.

"The mother has her sights set on other, less alien game. She considers me a foreign predator trifling with the affections of her only offspring. If the truth be told, she probably suspects me of practicing every vice known to mankind, including Sunday traveling. By God, I mean to prove her wrong."

As they walked on, Roderic wondered if Mrs. Gordon might not prove a helpful if unlikely ally in his campaign to separate the prince and her daughter. "Will I have the pleasure of meeting Mrs.

Gordon at the dinner party?" he asked.

Lothar shook his head. "I understand she decamped for Brighton several days ago, undoubtedly for a lengthy tryst of some sort with her latest paramour. But not without first recruiting a proxy dragon to leave behind to protect the fair Rowena."

"And who, pray tell, is this standin for Mrs. Gordon?"

"I have yet to have the misfortune of meeting the woman. Her name is Miss Celeste Prescott, she's a spinster without a penny to her name who hails from Southampton, and she's a bluestocking with a penchant for truth-telling, or so I was informed."

"Celeste Prescott." The name meant nothing to Roderic. As he turned it over on his tongue he found it neither pleasing nor displeasing. The image of the woman ushered into his mind by his friend's words, however, was distinctly unappealing.

"If you favored my courtship of Rowena," Lothar said, "I might suggest that you ingratiate yourself with this Miss Prescott and thus be of assistance to me. If you recall, you always had a knack for making yourself agreeable to ladies of that particular stripe. I expect they saw you as a rake in dire need of reformation."

Roderic nodded as Lothar's words sparked the first glimmerings of a scheme to separate the prince from Rowena Gordon. If only he was able to endure this Prescott woman's moralizings, and he supposed he could endure anything for a brief time at least, he might then, by means of a combination of blandishments, a series of small yet prized attentions, and subtle flattery, induce her to help him further their common goal of undermining Lothar's ill-conceived affair of the heart.

He drew in a deep, self-satisfied breath. Such a course would represent a sacrifice on his part, but confident that Miss Celeste Prescott would prove no match for Roderic Courtney-Trench, Earl of Campion, he was more than willing to make that sacrifice.

Chapter 5

There are few circumstances more unsettling to a member of the female sex than to find herself a guest at a glittering gathering in the heart of Mayfair garbed in last season's fashions.

A lady may momentarily forget the name of the country's prime minister without fear of serious rebuke; she may recommend a cure for the vapors that long ago fell into disfavor and expect to be forgiven; she may maintain that "The Blue Boy" was the work of Constable and still hold her head high after being proven wrong.

But to be forced to appear at a Mayfair dinner party in a skirt that almost sweeps the floor when all the other ladies attract the surreptitious and fascinated glances of the gentlemen by revealing a glimpse of their ankles; to be seen in a gown with short puffed sleeves when modish sleeves are now, without exception, long and narrow; or to be guilty of any one of a score of similar gaffes, is nothing less than devastating.

Even Celeste, who had never considered herself a slave to the whims of fashion, felt ill at ease when she entered Lord Appling's drawing room with Rowena. Her gown of white India muslin had the outmoded puffed sleeves, the long skirt, and a high décolletage while Rowena's lemon yellow silk gown, of Paris creation, managed to triumphantly avoid each of these blunders.

Their host, Lord Appling, a gruff yet gracious older gentleman, appeared unaware that Celeste failed to be quite the thing as performed his duties as a host by introducing her to his wife, Lucy, and then to the others of the intimate gathering—Mr. and Mrs. Richard Small and Prince Lothar. Lord Campion had, he explained, been unavoidably delayed.

The prince bowed over her hand, remarked on the unremarkable winter weather, and then proceeded to capture Rowena and bear his more than willing prisoner off to the window seat at the far side of the room.

"Rowena favors her Aunt Joan more than she does her mother," Lady Appling said.

"Quite right." Her husband nodded vehemently. "Or else her Aunt Jezebel. What do you think, Miss Prescott?"

Celeste was forced to admit she had never heard of either of the aunts.

"Of course not, they live in Scotland," Lady Appling explained.

"In Scotland," her husband repeated, adding, "In the vicinity of Glasgow, I do believe."

"Rowena and her prince make a charming couple," Lady Appling said.

"A charming couple, by God," her husband echoed.

Celeste could only agree. Rowena, with the bloom of youth in her cheeks, her grey eyes sparkling and her black ringlets spilling over a diadem of pearls, looked lovely. As for Lothar, she could understand how the boyish-looking prince, attired in the gold and white uniform of a Marien-Holstein colonel of the royal guard, would appeal to an older woman. Even Celeste would have been charmed if she knew nothing about his flawed character. Just as the devil was known to be adept at assuming disguises, she reminded herself, the devil's followers were undoubtedly also more than capable of deceiving the unwary.

And yet, watching Rowena with the prince, she couldn't avoid feeling a pang of envy. She had never known the bittersweet joys of love, either false or true, she had never waited breathlessly to learn whether her love would be returned, she had never looked at a man with obvious rapture as Rowena gazed at Prince Lothar.

She wondered if she ever would.

Celeste forced her attention back to Lady Appling, who was singing the praises of Marien-Holstein, while her husband served as a chorus of one, repeating her encomiums and occasionally adding his own variations. In conversation, Lady Appling escorted her husband through the thickets of pronunciation and the swamps of inappropriate subjects just as an experienced guide would lead a stranger across unfamiliar terrain.

Lord Appling had brought a heavy purse to the

marriage, Rowena had told her, while Lady Appling had supplied social position. As in most combinations of this sort, their union had succeeded in elevating him slightly while lowering her a great deal. Lady Appling was forced to be content with a salon that attracted mainly artists, poets, authors and foreigners, all of whom seemingly lacked the keen sensibilities of the cream of the *ton* who managed to tolerate Lord Appling because of his wealth without completely accepting him because of his antecedents, in particular his late father.

Lord Appling's father had had the misfortune of being In Trade. Although his resulting wealth, it was said by the envious, had led to his elevation to the peerage, his children and his children's children were fated to be looked at askance since they could not be expected to fully appreciate the importance of living a life exclusively devoted to mannered idleness. His inherited stigma of having been In Trade would be wiped clear only with the passing of at least two generations devoted to preserving civilized values by maintaining large establishments in town and in the country, visiting Bath and Brighton in season, engaging in clever conversations, playing whist, wagering on horse races and attending dinner parties, balls and masquerades dressed in the height of fashion.

Lord Appling, following the prudent guidance of his wife, never referred to the source of his wealth although it was widely and correctly whispered to be the Belvedere Shops, named for Lord Appling's widowed mother, Isabelle. These shops, centrally located in London and several of the other major

English cities, provided women with a wide selection of necessities including brushes, combs, mirrors, pins, scents, powders, salves, perfumed waters, hair dyes and breath sweeteners.

Lady Appling, after enumerating the blessings of Marien-Holstein to Celeste, had begun reviewing that kingdom's shortcomings when an extraordinary event occurred. As Celeste looked back on it later, the moment stood out in her mind with a startling yet perplexing clarity.

Lady Appling was lamenting Marien-Holstein's lack of profitable exports, Lord Appling now conversed with the Smalls—he was discussing the proposed Regent's Park—the fire crackled, the ormolu clock on the mantel showed the time to be exactly ten minutes before eight, Rowena was sitting in the window seat gazing up at Prince Lothar while through the window beyond the couple large white snowflakes began to drift down past the gas light on the street outside.

An unnatural hush fell on the room; time itself seemed suspended. A tingle of expectancy swept over Celeste, the same feeling she had experienced during her few visits to the theatre as the audience grew quiet and the curtain parted, that instant when reality is held in abeyance waiting for fantasy to begin weaving its enchanting web.

She glanced up and saw a man's face and shoulders perfectly framed in the oval mirror above the fireplace mantel. Lord Campion, it could be no other, had arrived unannounced, and now paused in the doorway dressed in a coat of midnight blue, a strand of his jet hair falling over his forehead, his dark, handsome face flushed by the cold of the February night.

As she watched, Lord Campion at first frowned as though he suspected he was being observed and then glanced across the room into the mirror, his brown eyes meeting and holding hers. He looked away almost at once but not before she shivered with a thrill of recognition that puzzled her, since she was certain she had never set eyes on him before.

Cautiously, she looked about her to see if anyone had noticed her inexplicable reaction. Evidently no one had, for Lady Appling still talked of imports and exports, Lord Appling was crossing the room, his hand extended to greet his guest, and the others were as yet unaware of Lord Campion's presence.

Campion would now come to her at once; Celeste had no doubt of his coming to her and the knowledge flustered her. With the warmth she felt, inexplicable though it was, how should she act toward him? Perhaps she should exhibit an indifferent friendliness. Or should she retreat even further and be aloof and distant? Whatever course she selected, she feared she'd be unable to calm her tremulous heart in time to behave other than foolishly.

But Lord Campion did not come to her. He talked briefly with Lord Appling, he was introduced to the Smalls and listened with polite attention to Mrs. Small's account of the rigors of a visit to her parents in Bath while accompanied by their five children. At first Celeste was annoyed at him for deliberately ignoring her but almost at once her annoyance turned against herself for becoming irritated by the seeming indifference of this man she held in such poor regard.

Though she had been comfortable a few minutes before, now the room seemed much too warm. She closed her eyes, afraid of being overcome by dizziness. She must be coming down with some ailment, she told herself; yes, that was the cause of her lightheadedness, the damp February nights had given her *la grippe.* This common sensical explanation made her sigh with relief.

Now, she noted, Lord Campion was conversing with Lothar, as Rowena, listening with rapt attention, every so often glanced up with evident admiration at the prince's friend. She really must warn Rowena to better veil her emotions, especially from men. Didn't she, after all, carry a fan for just such a purpose?

With a slight start, Celeste realized what Lord Campion must have in mind. He was coming to her after first circling the room to satisfy the demands of etiquette, briefly speaking to each of the guests while reserving her for the last. Yes, here he was now, deftly separating her from Lady Appling as soon as they had been introduced, bowing over her hand, drawing her to one side away from the others.

Disconcertingly, as soon as they were alone together he said nothing to her for what seemed an eternity but was probably only a minute or two. His dark brooding appearance reminded her of a portrait of his friend Lord Byron, now in Italy after fleeing England in a swirl of scandal the year before. Lord Campion's eyes, she noticed, were the color of topaz but each contained a wedge of a lighter amber shade. She had an urge, quickly suppressed, to push the errant strand of dark hair from his forehead.

"I was mistaken," he said, breaking the silence.

He must have thought he recognized her. "No," she told him, "we have never met before."

"You felt it, too, then. But no, not that. When I arrived I stood on the walk outside watching the snow beginning to fall." He paused. "I love the snow," he said, almost as though to himself. "It changes everything, softens what was drear, makes you believe a better world is possible. And then it melts into slush."

He shook his head as though to rouse himself from his reverie. "I happened to glance through the drawing room window and saw you. The glass was frosted, your image was unclear, so I told myself, no, she can't be as lovely as you think. And then I stood in the doorway to this room and saw you again, reflected in the mirror, and I said, no, the glass distorts her image. But now that I see you face to face, I realize I was mistaken, and you *are* as lovely as I imagined when first I saw you through the frosted window."

A vivid flush tinged her face. Stepping away from him, she shook her head as she raised her fan. He had met her only a few minutes ago and already he was making love to her. All she had heard about him must have been true; her first impression, that his words were meant for her and her alone, had been false. Lord Campion would flatter any woman with the same glittering falsehoods.

"I was warned in Guildford," she said, "that in London I would be apt to encounter gentlemen who rise before ten in the morning merely to spend an hour to two polishing their collection of *bon mots,* anecdotes and, of course, their outrageous compliments."

"You do me an grave injustice, Miss Prescott. I was informed"—he glanced across the room at Prince Lothar—"how much you valued the truth and so I vowed that I would tell you only what I believed in my heart to be true."

Perhaps he wouldn't flatter just any woman, perhaps he had a special reason for complimenting her. "Informed by Prince Lothar, I expect," she said. When he nodded, she went on, "Prince Lothar, your very dear friend."

"He has been that since the day we met. Although on occasion we find ourselves at odds, I always have his best interests at heart. As he has mine."

No, he might not flatter just any woman, she decided, but certainly any woman who might help advance his friend Lothar's courtship of Rowena Gordon. As she could. His ploy was obvious; fortunately she had discerned the intent of his over-effusive compliments before it was too late to guard against them.

". . . the masquerade at Darlington House?"

She blinked as she tried to recall what he had asked her. Whether she planned to attend the masquerade, yes, that was the gist of his question. "I have been invited," she said, "and plan to attend with Rowena."

"May I suggest you disguise yourself as a princess? Nothing less would do you justice. The only disadvantage would be that everyone would think you a real princess who had failed to disguise herself."

Pleasure surged through her until cool reason intruded. Lord Campion, she reminded herself, could embark on the most outrageous flights of fancy with what appeared to be complete sincerity. She had best put him his place at once by showing him that his flattery had absolutely no effect on her.

"I would hesitate to masquerade as a princess," she informed him. "What of Lothar? Might he not become alarmed, thinking I might be a certain Bavarian princess come to London to insist that he fulfill his vows?"

"I believe his so-called betrothal is more form than substance."

"I might have more faith in your words, Lord Campion, if I understood their precise meaning."

"By all means let me define them for you." An edge of irritation sharpened his voice. "Prince Lothar has never made any vows to any princess, Bavarian or otherwise, and he has no intention of doing so."

"Since the prince is betrothed to Princess Hildegarde, may I in turn provide you with a definition. I understand betrothal to be a mutual contract for a future marriage. It appears one of us must be mistaken."

"In any dispute between myself and a lady, regardless of the right or the wrong, it has always been my policy to defer to the lady." He smiled. "In this case, however, I make an exception. You, Miss Prescott, should ascertain all the facts before leaping to a conclusion."

"I was about to say the same to you, my lord."

He reached to her and touched the back of her gloved hand with his fingertips. She drew in her breath as, looking up at his handsome face made taut with anger, she sensed the threat of violence lurking behind his facade of gentlemanly behavior.

He lowered his voice. "Why are you so vexed, Miss Prescott?" he demanded. "Are you laying your grievance against the world at my feet? Surely nothing I have done could account for your hostility."

"Nothing you did today, perhaps." Finding that if she met his intent gaze, her thoughts became hopelessly muddled, she looked past him at a painting of the English countryside on the wall. "The twig—Lothar—was bent years ago," she said, "and today the tree grows crooked and nothing we can do now has the power to change it. You were the teacher, Lothar was the student, he learned his profligate ways from you, he learned to be deceitful from you, he learned to use guile from you, he learned—"

His fingers tightened on her wrist. "This will not do," he said. Leaning to her until he was so close she felt his breath on her lips, he said, "Enough!"

She stared at him, frozen with apprehension and with something else she was unable to name. Suddenly he relaxed, releasing her and stepping away as the corner of his mouth twitched in a sardonic smile. "When Lothar told me about you, I hoped we might join forces," he said. "I see the impossibility of that. When I met you this evening I thought, perhaps—" He sighed, shook his head, then offered her his arm.

Puzzled, she frowned.

"I believe dinner has been announced," he said, "and our host has informed me I have the pleasure of escorting you, Miss Prescott, to the festive board." He placed the slightest emphasis on the word "pleasure."

Taking his arm, she entered the dining room with him and soon found herself sitting opposite him. All during the dinner of capons stuffed with truffles that followed and, later, when the gentlemen rejoined the ladies in the drawing room, he behaved toward her with a meticulous politeness. She wondered if she had been imprudent in rejecting him, too hasty by half, wondered what he had meant by their joining forces. And, more intriguingly, what else had he thought possible?

Much later, as she lay in her high four-poster bed at the Gordon's, listening to the snow whispering at the window as she waited for elusive sleep to come, she reviewed the events of the evening. She had been perfectly right in spurning him, she assured herself, even in being the least bit rude since Lord Campion was a man she could never trust.

Be honest with yourself, an inner voice insisted. *Admit the truth: where Lord Campion is concerned, the one you can't trust is yourself.*

Chapter 6

The snow was still falling fitfully when Celeste awakened the following morning. All during breakfast she and Rowena watched the large fluffy flakes twirl past the windows to the ground.

When the snow stopped shortly before noon, Rowena ran to a window, flung it open and looked down at a world of white. Turning to Celeste, her face flushed from the cold, she asked, "Can you remember frolicking in the snow when you were a girl?"

Celeste nodded.

"Shall we?" A youthful excitement danced in Rowena's voice.

"Yes!"

They hurried to fetch their clothes, bundled themselves in coats and hats and scarves, pulled on boots and mittens as unobtrusive servants watched, smiling indulgently. They met in the vestibule, eyes glittering; Rowena opened the front door and they stood side by side staring out at an unfamiliar city.

Wet snow clung to the bare branches of the trees in the square creating delicate traceries of white and black. Snow mounded on the iron railings of the fences, on the Gordon's hitching post, on the stepping stone, on the roofs and chimneys of the houses across the way. As yet there were no tracks in front of the house where the snow covered the road to a depth of several inches. Two doors along the street a houseman shoveled the front walk while a maid swept the steps.

Celeste and Rowena ran to the far side of the square, their breath pluming in the crisp, cold air, laughing as they scooped snow into their hands and threw it at one another. They lay side by side on the ground, sweeping their arms up and down to make angels, they played joyfully in the snow until, giddy, tired and damp, they walked slowly, hand in hand, back toward the house.

What a good time they had had, Celeste thought. Already she considered the younger woman her friend. Now, more than ever, she was determined to do everything in her power to save her from heartbreak.

"La, such fun," Rowena said, "I love the winter, the cold, the snow. I remember another winter three years ago when the river froze from bank to bank and my mother's—" She hesitated in embarrassed confusion before going on. "When my mother's gentleman friend escorted us to the Frost Fair. All manner of shops were set up on the ice along what they called Freezeland Street, there were swings and peddlers, a skittle alley and a wheel of fortune and oysters and brandyballs and gingerbread to eat. Such a wonderful time we had then!"

"When I was at school in Guildford," Celeste said, "I could hardly wait to grow up."

"And now you wish you were a child again."

"At times I do," she admitted.

"Men are the ones who make life complicated." Rowena, so gay and animated only moments before, seemed to droop. "Last evening, Lothar told me his uncle, the king, sent Lord Campion here for the express purpose of discouraging Lothar's interest in me."

Surprised, Celeste turned to Rowena. "Discouraging him? Are you certain?"

"Quite certain. Though Lothar assures me he has no intention of blindly doing Campion's bidding. Lothar will act as he sees fit." Though Rowena nodded emphatically, Celeste detected a thread of worry in her voice. "He is, after all, a prince."

"What objection does the king have?"

Rowena's mouth tightened. "King Harlan cares not a whit for Lothar's happiness, all he desires for him is a marriage that will benefit Marien-Holstein. That, at least, is his stated reason. Actually, I suspect they think he lowers himself by marrying me. And"—for a moment Celeste thought her friend would break into tears—"he may have other objections. To my family, to my not having a father and so forth and so on."

What could she mean, Celeste wondered. Since the lack of a father hardly seemed a legitimate hindrance to marriage, even marriage to a prince, she wondered if Rowena was concealing something. She made no comment, however, and they resumed their walk back to the Gordon house.

"Not that I blame Lord Campion," Rowena said, "since he only knows what he's been told. As soon as he realizes the truth of the matter, his stance will change." She lowered her voice. "Didn't you find Campion dashing? And just a trifle world-weary, much like Lord Byron must have been. If my heart wasn't already claimed by Lothar—" She left the thought unfinished.

Celeste smiled to herself. How easily impressed Rowena (and others, as well, she supposed) was by a handsome face and a surface charm. How surprised he must have been when she, Celeste, gave him a setdown. On the other hand, now that she knew what Campion must have meant by joining forces, she wondered if she had been too hasty in rebuffing him. No, she decided, they were too different to be able to work well together, she would have to let matters rest exactly where they were.

A lone horseman passed them; Celeste noted there were now carriage tracks on the street even though the horse-drawn plows had not yet made their appearance. At the Gordon's, a houseboy, his breath pluming in the cold, was using a coal shovel to clear the walk.

Inside the house, no sooner had they shed their wraps than Harkins approached Rowena bearing a letter on a silver tray. She slit open the seal and, her face aglow, began reading the message.

"La, what fun it will be, we must go." She looked up from the letter at Celeste. "This afternoon at two," she said. "Lothar proposes to drive the two of us into the country in his tilbury."

"Will Lord Campion be with him?" Celeste asked without thinking.

When Rowena gave her a questioning look, she felt the color rise to her face. "I asked because I do not care overmuch to be in his company," she said hastily. Which was no more than the truth. Wasn't it?

Rowena shook her head. "He makes no mention of Lord Campion." Folding the letter, she carefully tucked it into her pocket. "Lothar is quite mysterious about the purpose of our excursion. He insists more than mere pleasure is involved, in fact he claims a great opportunity has unfolded that he means to seize forthwith though what the opportunity is he fails to say."

Remembering the prince's reputation for possessing the usually fatal combination of optimism, poor judgment and profligacy, Celeste could only groan to herself.

"You must wear your scarlet coat and your Russian fur hat," Rowena said a short while later as they sat sipping cocoa while warming themselves before the fire in the drawing room. "Both are quite the thing."

Celeste agreed, having discovered that her outer winter garb had weathered the swift changes in fashion much better than her gowns. That Lord Campion would not have the opportunity to see her in these more attractive clothes, she assured herself, was of no concern. She wasn't in the least disappointed by his failure to accompany the prince, in fact, the drive into the country would be much more pleasant without him.

Prince Lothar arrived alone in his tilbury shortly

after two and, scarves wrapped about their necks and carriage robes drawn up around them, they set off. Celeste, savoring the bite of the cool air on her face, glanced from side to side as they drove north, admiring the brown and red chimney pots on the Baker Street roofs vividly outlined against the brilliant blue of the sky.

They turned onto the New Road from Paddington, driving toward Islington, the sound of hooves and wheels muffled though here the snow had either been trampled down or mostly cleared. When they swung north onto Albany Street they found the road less traveled, the deeper snow forcing them to slow their pace. They were in the country now with farm houses and cow sheds to their right, low hills ahead, and farmland on their left, the fields divided by hedge rows of shrubs with, here and there, a lone tree.

"What a marvelous vista!" Lothar cried. "One day very soon," he told Celeste, "the Prince Regent and John Nash, his architect, will bring the world's greatest park into being on this very spot. They plan to build magnificent villas, a serpentine lake and gardens containing all manner of botanical wonders."

Celeste warmed to his enthusiasm. Though perhaps naive and overly optimistic, his infectious boyish charm and his ready smile made her understand why Rowena felt a tenderness for him.

"A new thoroughfare from Westminster," he told them, "will bring the town within a short ride or walk from the terraces of houses to be constructed around the edges of the park. The Prince Regent is even building a canal from Limehouse to the north.

London will never be the same again!"

"There are those who object to the expense," Celeste ventured.

"Princes must devise on a grand scale," Lothar said, "for if they do not, who will? Haggling over the pennies and the pounds is the province of parliaments. A hundred years from today Regent's Park will stand as a dazzling monument to the Prince while the naysayers and the pennypinchers will have been long forgotten."

Celeste remained unconvinced, wondering if upheavals such as the French Revolution had been protests against similar grandiose notions.

"Does the great opportunity you mentioned in your letter," Rowena asked the prince, "involve the Park?"

"I see I *have* aroused your curiosity." Lothar smiled enigmatically. "Be patient, my dear Rowena, in good time all will be revealed."

When, minutes later, she heard Lothar murmur an almost inaudible "Aha," Celeste followed his gaze, the glare of the sun reflecting from the virgin snow forcing her to narrow her eyes. A short distance ahead the tracks of a horse led away from the road, climbed a small hill and disappeared over the top.

Lothar reined his horse to a stop. Standing in the carriage and shielding his eyes from the sun, he gazed at the nearby hill and shouted, "Halloo!" There was no reply. "Mr. Wyche!" he called. Still there was no reply.

Lothar leaped to the snow-covered ground. "Wait in the carriage," he told them, "I'll find him in a trice."

"Please, Lothar," Rowena said, "allow me to go with you, I intend to miss nothing." She glanced at Celeste. "And you?" she asked. Celeste nodded.

"Then you both must come."

After handing them down from the carriage, Lothar walked ahead to trample a path through the snow. When they reached the crest of the hill, Celeste looked down the other side and saw a rider wearing a dark many-caped coat, his back to them, sitting astride his horse a short distance away.

He reminded her of Napolean, Celeste thought, recalling a picture of the French emperor surveying a battlefield from horseback. When the stranger, in answer to Lothar's cry of delighted recognition, reined his horse toward them, the impression vanished as she saw that he was short and rather stout, his hair was carrot-colored, his oval face florid.

"This is Mr. Wyche," Lothar told them.

Wyche dismounted, removed his hat and swept it in front of him as he executed an extravagent bow. "Samuel Wyche at your service," he said. "Wyche rhymes with rich."

"And is this the land?" Lothar asked eagerly after introducing Rowena and Celeste.

Wyche turned slightly and extended his arms, palms down, as though blessing the expanse of farmland below them. "Aye, Prince Lothar," he said, "and teeming with promise for a gentleman of vision such as yourself."

"It appears to be all you claimed," Lothar said.

Wyche nodded. Turning to Rowena and Celeste, he said, "Has the prince explained our enterprise to you? Our proposed company?"

They shook their heads in unison.

"You may, then, have many questions so allow me attempt to attempt to anticipate them. 'How did you discover this magnificent opportunity?' you might ask. Allow me to explain my methodology. 'In what direction is London growing?' was the first query I put to myself. 'For the most part,' I answered, 'to the north.' I therefore made a series of excursions in that direction, waiting until I came upon land offered for sale not by the individual lot but by the acre. At that point, standing where we now stand, my search was over.

"You, sir," he said to Lothar, "undoubtedly prefer residing in the bustle of the city while you, madam," he added with a glance at Celeste, "may well favor the tranquility of the country. Here you have the best of both worlds: a convenient drive to town while residing amidst serene vistas of rural living."

Who did Mr. Wyche remind her of, Celeste wondered. The answer was not long in coming. He possessed the same facile fervor as Mr. Morland, her former guardian who had absconded with her father's fortune. Prince Lothar had best beware.

Mr. Wyche went on extolling the virtues of the site, picturing semi-detached houses built on gently curving streets but, at some point, Celeste stopped listening. When Wyche led the others a short distance away to admire another vista, she remained where she was.

A sudden breeze sent snow whirling around her, dampening her face. Mr. Wyche's voice faded, she stood alone beneath heaven's dome of blue with the pristine snow stretching away on all sides. In the distance the spires of London rose into the clear and cloudless sky. Lowering her gaze, she noticed a black speck—she assumed it was a carriage—leaving the New Road to drive in her direction.

She gazed as though bewitched across the great expanse of white where only the single dark speck moved, growing larger and larger until she could distinguish a black horse drawing not a carriage but a sleigh. When the sleigh came to the spot where Lothar had left his tilbury, she heard the jingle of bells. Not pausing, the sleigh veered from the road, following their tracks up the hill and stopping a few feet from her.

Lord Campion leaped to the ground. She stared at him, breathless.

"I drove here as soon as I heard," he said. "Lothar neglected to tell me."

At first she thought he meant he had come to her. No, he must have driven here to discover the truth about Lothar's great opportunity. How featherheaded of her to imagine, even for a moment, that he had any interest in her other than to further his own attempts to discourage Lothar's interest in Rowena.

"Mr. Samuel Wyche," she said, nodding toward the others who remained unaware of Campion's arrival, "is describing a speculation, the buying of land near the Regent's Park and the building of houses. I believe Prince Lothar intends to invest with him."

Lord Campion started to speak, stopped, shook his head in dismay.

"Will you attempt to dissuade him?" she asked.

"Not now but I will later, in private. Though of

late the prince has been singularly disinclined to follow my advice. I must admit I find his attitude rather discomfiting though more befitting a prince." He looked at her in a speaking way. "My powers of persuasion have failed with others as well."

She reddened. "When we spoke last night I believed you favored their match."

"Not at all. Any liaison between Lothar and Miss Rowena Gordon will only encourage the prince's worst inclinations."

"Admit the truth, my lord. Your prince is probably beyond saving."

Smiling slightly, he held up his hand as though suing for a truce. "Wherever the fault may lie, Miss Prescott, we two have identical goals. I suggest, as I attempted to do last evening, that we join forces to thwart the match. I propose that you and I become partners."

Unwilling to be hurried to a decision, she asked, "How would you proceed?"

"My first approach would be to devise a scheme that would demonstrate to both of them how misguided any alliance would be."

She wanted to agree to help him, yet she hesitated. This man, she realized, meant to employ whatever trickery he thought necessary to achieve his ends. Not only would he deceive Lothar and Rowena, he would also deceive her if it suited his purpose.

And he had the power, she admitted reluctantly, ruefully, to hurt her terribly if she wasn't very, very careful.

Before she could decide how to answer, Lothar hailed Campion and a moment later the prince and the others joined them. "Pray allow Mr. Wyche to describe his plans," he said to Campion.

"No, later if you please. I must return to town."

Lothar nodded. "We shall race to the New Road then," he proposed. "My tilbury against your sleigh for ten guineas."

"The sleigh's better suited to the snow. And you have reason to know Blaze's speed. I suggest you assign me a handicap."

"See that tree." Lothar pointed along the road in the direction of town. "Wait until I pass the tree before you begin."

"Fair enough."

"Miss Prescott must accompany you, Roderic. To even the weights."

"Agreed."

Before Celeste could protest, Lothar offered Rowena his arm and they set off on foot to the carriage. Lord Campion helped her into the sleigh while Mr. Wyche, who had remounted his horse, watched from nearby.

"I sense a hesitation," Lord Campion said as he sat beside her. "Are you afraid?"

She frowned, puzzled. "Of riding with you in your sleigh?"

"No, afraid of being my partner."

She refused to lie to him. "Yes, I am," she admitted.

Instead of attempting to reassure her, he merely nodded, then turned from her to flick the reins. As they circled toward the road, she glanced ahead and saw the tilbury passing the designated tree about a quarter of a mile ahead of them. When they jounced from the field to the road, their bodies touched briefly, and, though she drew away at once, she felt oddly breathless as well as acutely aware of his presence.

Once on the road, Lord Campion urged his horse into a trot. "Blaze is slow to start but fast to finish," he told her.

At first they failed to gain on the prince and Rowena; disappointed, Celeste told herself they could never overtake them. Campion snapped the whip, called Blaze's name, and she felt their pace increase, the horse galloping, snow flying back at them from the thudding hooves. They hurtled on, faster and faster, the sleigh swooshing over the snow, bells jangling wildly, Blaze's hooves throbbing like her own quickened heartbeats.

One would think, she reproved herself, that she'd never ridden in a sleigh before. Yet this ride was different for one reason and one reason only: he rode beside her, heightening each of her sensations, her keen delight in their speed, her zest from the feel of the crisp cold bite of the wind and her rising excitement as she listened to the pulsating hoofbeats.

Slowly they closed on the tilbury, finally drew even and raced alongside. Glancing to her left, she saw Prince Lothar urge his horse to greater effort, heard Rowena cry out her encouragement, and then they were past them, the sleigh steadily drawing away.

Lord Campion shouted in triumph.

She gripped the side railing as they raced toward the turn into the New Road. Their pace never slackened. Too fast, too fast, she murmured under her breath while at the same time she exulted in their speed. At last, with the New Road upon them, Lord Campion drew back on the reins, the horse slowed and turned to the right, the sleigh slewed sideways across the road, tilted precariously and overturned, throwing them onto the snow in a jumble of arms and legs, tumbling over and over, at last coming to rest in a bank of snow with Lord Campion sprawled on top of her.

He pushed himself up on one elbow. His breath warm on her cheek, he asked anxiously, "Are you hurt?"

All too aware of the intimacy of their position, she tested her arms and legs. "No," she told him.

How reckless Campion was. He'd blithely taken her on a dangerous drive, risked her life as well as his. Yet she had enjoyed every moment.

He stared down at her, the glow in his eyes sending a thrill tingling through her. For an instant she thought he meant to lean toward her and . . . breathless with anticipation, she closed her eyes.

He sprang to his feet, reached down, took her hands in his and pulled her up to stand facing him.

"Partners?" he asked. "The two of us?"

Telling herself firmly that she was not in the least disappointed, she nodded and said, "Yes, partners."

Chapter 7

During the days that followed, London's soot blackened the snow's surface while at the same time mild breezes from the southwest turned much of the snow and ice into a slush that froze at night only to thaw in the morning. What had been a wondrously white world of fantasy became a depressing reminder of an often drab reality.

Celeste soon became aware that Rowena had more than the weather to plague her. Late one morning while they sat readingin the drawing room, Rowena received a letter in the post. After scanning the message, she thrust the letter into her pocket and then rose to pace back and forth in front of the fire while shaking her head in consternation.

Celeste was certain the disquieting letter came from Prince Lothar. The day before, Rowena had told her the prince intended to invest a considerable sum in Mr. Wyche's land speculation. Lord Campion, she reported, had argued vehemently against the project, but to no avail. Celeste wondered if the letter brought word of a sudden turn for the worse in the prince's fortunes.

She looked questioningly at Rowena. Her friend stopped pacing and seemed about to speak only to abruptly shake her head, burst into tears and run sobbing from the room. How terrible for her, Celeste thought, starting to rise and follow her only to sink back into her chair, afraid of seeming presumptuous. If Rowena wanted her to know the cause of her dismay, she would find an occasion to tell her.

Two days went by. Although Rowena had quickly regained her composure, she remained deep in the doldrums and, despite many opportunities, never referred to the unsettling letter. At this uneasy juncture, another perturbing event occurred.

Again they were in the drawing room, though this afternoon found Celeste working on her embroidery while Rowena did needlepoint. A few minutes after the long clock in the hall struck two, Celeste frowned and looked up, certain she'd smelled the acrid odor of smoke.

She glanced at the hearth fire, lit against the chill of the day. The draught was good and the flames leaped high; there was no sign the smoke came from the fireplace. Since the lamps weren't lit, they couldn't be the source. With rising alarm, Celeste looked to the hall door and gasped when she saw a wisp of smoke curl wraith-like into the room.

"Rowena," she said, attempting to keep her voice calm, "I fear there must be a fire somewhere in the house."

Rowena raised her head, drew in a breath and, eyes widening in alarm, sprang to her feet, her needlepoint falling to the floor. "My room," she cried, "I must reach my room." She ran toward the door.

"Wait." Celeste started after her. "We should go outside at once."

Rowena shook her head but before she reached the door it was flung open and Harkins appeared. When he saw them he raised both hands. "Ladies," he said, "you must calm yourselves. There's no cause for alarm, no cause at all."

"But the smoke—" Celeste began.

"Merely a faulty flue in the kitchen," Harkins assured them. "Joseph is on his way to fetch the chimney sweep while Millie opens the windows." He frowned. "I don't rightly understand it; we had the chimneys cleaned in August. If Fogarty asks for so much as a penny for setting them to rights, he'll find himself whistling in the wind."

Celeste shivered as a gust of clear chill air blew through the open hall door.

"It might be wise for you ladies to repair to your rooms," Harkins said, "'til the smoke clears."

Celeste had no sooner settled herself at the desk in her bed chamber, intending to write first to Miss Argent and then to Mrs. Gordon, when there was a tapping at her door and Rowena entered holding a small framed picture clasped to her bosom.

When she placed the picture on the desk, Celeste recognized the watercolor miniature as a portrait of Prince Lothar in uniform astride a rearing black charger, his sword raised to lead a cavalry charge.

"When first I feared there was a fire," Rowena told her, "my only thought was to save this portrait, Lothar's gift to me on my eighteenth birthday." As

Rowena gazed down at the portrait, tears welled in her eyes. "Never will we be one," she murmured despairingly, "never, never."

Celeste clasped her friend's hand. "Nothing is impossible." As soon as she spoke she experienced a twinge of guilt. How could she encourage Rowena at the same time she attempted to thwart her? Her heart went out to Rowena, she felt her distress as acutely as if it were her own, even while reason assured her she had acted properly in agreeing to join forces with Lord Campion. Though she had heard nothing more from him she was certain he had no intention of giving up his campaign to separate Rowena and the prince.

Almost as though sensing Celeste's ambivalence, Rowena drew her hand away, snatched up the miniature and walked to the fireplace. For a moment, Celeste thought she meant to hurl the picture into the flames but, still holding it, Rowena covered her eyes with one hand and sobbed. "How can something so true and right be so hopeless?" she asked.

Celeste rose and went to her, embracing and soothing her as Rowena buried her head on Celeste's shoulder. At last, her sobs subsiding, Rowena drew away, sighed, then turned and walked slowly to the window. With her back to Celeste, she said, her voice a disheartened monotone, "The letter I received on Tuesday came from mama. She returns from Brighton for a few days' visit to attend the masquerade. Mama always succeeds in making an appearance at the most inopportune of times."

Though surprised that Mrs. Gordon intended to return from Brighton, Celeste failed to understand why the news had so unsettled Rowena.

"Lothar gives every evidence of having a great tenderness for me," Rowena explained. "I have no doubt he loves me, yet he has never declared for me. For one reason more than any other—my mother."

"I found no fault with her. She appeared a perfectly respectable matron."

Rowena uttered a sound that could have been either a laugh or a sob. She turned from the window, the miniature clutched in one hand, a handkerchief in the other. When she spoke, rather than looking at Celeste she stared down at the floor. "Then she appeared to be precisely what she is not. My mother is infamous for having lived under the protection of a succession of gentlemen ever since the death of my father."

Celeste stared at her friend, aghast. She felt compassion for Rowena; if what she said were true, and there was no reason to doubt her, any suitable match for her was improbable while marriage to the prince was well-nigh impossible. Celeste herself felt betrayed since if she had known the truth she would never have accepted a position in Mrs. Gordon's household.

"Mama has no idea I know," Rowena said. "All these years she's lied to me, hiding the truth while the world snickered at her while laughing at me behind my back. I only discovered the truth last summer, and then by chance."

"Does the prince know?"

"Most certainly he does, even though, gentleman that he is, neither by word or deed has he given evidence of his knowledge."

"I had no notion your mother was other than she appeared."

"Now that you do know, will you leave me? Please don't, Celeste."

"Of course I won't. You can't be held responsible for your mother's indiscretions. No one should cast aspersions on you."

"They will, however; in fact, they do." She sighed. "It happens, by the bye, that her gentlemen friends are usually in the political arena. At least," she said bitterly, "or so some wit is reported to have remarked, she possesses a modicum of discrimination, since she prefers members of the House of Lords to the Commons." Rowena dabbed at the tears on her cheek. "Oh, Celeste, what am I to do? Help me, Celeste."

"Tell Lothar the truth," Celeste said without a moment's hesitation, "and then never see him again. The sooner you break with him the easier it will be for you. And not only for you, for him as well."

"Celeste, have you ever been in love? Truly, deeply in love? The first time I saw him I felt a flutter of my heart and ever after I find myself eager to hear others speak his name, to say his name myself. I burst into song at the oddest moments, I long to hear the sound of his step on the walk or the special intonation of his voice in a crowded room and I tremble when I do hear them. I love him, I could never give him up, no matter what may happen if I don't. There is nothing I would deny him, nothing."

Celeste, given pause by Rowena's passionate avowal, could only ask, "And does Prince Lothar return your love in equal measure?"

Rowena blushed. "Words come easily to Lothar. He professes to love me as I love him and I believe him. Would he give up everything for me, surrender his place in the royal family, renounce Marien-Holstein as he might have to if he married me?" She sighed. "He might truly believe he would, he might swear to me he would, but if the time actually came—"

"I never realized you saw him so clearly."

"Because you believe all who love are blind? Because he gambles recklessly and I never raise the slightest objection? Because he heeds the honeyed words of a mountebank such as Mr. Samuel Wyche while I do nothing to dissuade him? I suspect I see him clearly enough yet I dare not oppose him and thus risk giving him still another reason to listen to Lord Campion and his other friends who constantly advise him to turn his back on me."

"I'm so sorry," Celeste said, "both for you and for Lothar."

Rowena went to her and kissed her on the forehead. "How plaintive I must sound! Thank you for listening. I had to talk to someone and who better than my best friend in all the world?"

It was true, Celeste told herself, they were best friends though they'd known each other for only a few weeks. Somehow she must find a way to help Rowena, some way to induce her to stop seeing Lothar before she was even more grievously wounded.

"Talk to me whenever you wish," Celeste said. "About whatever you wish."

Walking to the door, Rowena turned before

leaving the room and, with the hint of a smile, said, "And if you ever desire to talk to *me* about anything, Lord Campion for instance, pray do so."

"Lord Campion?"

"I do believe both you and Lord Campion fail to listen to your hearts."

Celeste stared after Rowena, wondering what she meant. That she and Lord Campion evidenced a tenderness for each other? She shook her head. Impossible!

Her main concern must be Rowena, not herself. Now it was more important than ever to break the bond between Rowena and the prince. Not only did Rowena risk heartbreak, her love for the prince could only lead to disgrace and perhaps disaster. She'd been right, Celeste told herself, to agree to join Lord Campion in disrupting the alliance. Extreme measures were called for.

What scheme did Lord Campion have in mind, if any? Since more than a week had passed without a word from him, she wondered if he meant to wait until the night of the masquerade to lay his plans before her.

Once more she attempted to direct her thoughts to Rowena's dilemma but against her bidding they returned to Lord Campion. Closing her eyes, she smiled as she recalled the day she had met him, reliving the moment she glanced up to see his face framed in the oval mirror. Her pulses speeded when she pictured their next meeting followed by the wild dash through the snow and the thrilling glint in his eyes when he helped her to her feet after their spill on the New Road.

A loud rap startled her from her reverie. Looking up she saw the chimney sweep in the doorway of her bed chamber, a tall, soot-faced figure garbed in black. He wore a battered top hat and carried with him an array of implements including an assortment of brushes, a broom and a coil of rope looped at his waist.

The sweep strode across the room to the fireplace while motioning her with a dirty hand to remain where she was. "In and out I'll be, ma'am," he promised, "done in a flash."

She started to rise, then settled back in her chair as the sweep rattled the flue lever. "A splendid piece of construction, this fireplace, I must say," he remarked as much to himself as to her. To Celeste, the plain yellow brick supporting an oak mantle appeared little above the ordinary.

The sweep used the poker to send sparks from the fire dancing up the chimney. With a nod of satisfaction, he replaced the poker before turning and letting his gaze wander about the bed chamber. "An elegant room, I must say."

Celeste frowned, surprised by the familiarity of the comment even though her chamber, done in gold and cream with draperies of celestial blue, *was* elegant. Perhaps he thought he spoke to a servant. Actually, she reminded herself, that was precisely her position in the Gordon household although she seldom thought of herself as one.

The sweep removed his tall hat and held it clasped to his chest. "And you, miss," he said, "are splendid, as elegant and fetching a lady as ever I did see."

She rose to her feet, eyes flashing. "Sir," she said

with all the icy dignity she could muster, "you forget your place."

"Not so." He stepped toward her. She drew back. He came closer, smiled and, looking at him more closely, she found herself staring into the unique brown eyes of Lord Campion.

As soon as she recovered her composure enough to be able to speak, she stammered, "You—you must leave at once."

He shrugged and crossed to the open doorway where, instead of departing, he closed the door. "Pray allow me but a moment," he said with what she took to be a wicked glint in his eyes. Flabbergasted, she shook her head and started to reply but before she could speak he went on, "And let me remind you, Miss Prescott, no one need know I am here unless you create a hullabaloo. And in the future no one will ever know unless you tell them."

"You're—you're daft." She flung the word at him. "And too devious by half."

He smiled crookedly. "I much prefer being thought clever rather than devious. My chimney sweep disguise not only put me to considerable inconvenience but the expenditure of several pounds sterling as well. And all for the purpose"—he reached into a voluminous pocket of his sweep's coat and produced a small object neatly wrapped in blue rice paper—"of bringing you this gift."

Taken off guard, Celeste could only stare first at the proffered gift and then at him.

"Two days ago," he said, "I returned to my lodgings following dinner and came upon a wooden crate waiting for me just inside the front door. Upon examining the labels, I discovered it had been sent some weeks before from the king's palace in Marienhaven. Since I expected nothing from Marien-Holstein, you can well imagine my curiosity. I pried the crate open and inside found exactly one hundred of these." He placed his gift on the desk in front of her and stepped back, watching her with an air of expectancy. "I assure you, Miss Prescott, much as I might desire to offer you a gift of far greater value, I have exercised discretion in giving you something any lady could accept from a gentleman without compromising herself in the least."

When she folded her arms, ignoring his gift, he said, "The sooner you unwrap my small token, the sooner will I feel free to leave your chamber."

What gall he has, she thought. She glared at him, a long moment passed, and then with an indignant sigh she capitulated. Picking up the oval object, she couldn't resist holding it up to breathe in the scent she could smell through the paper.

"Lilacs," he told her.

Angry at herself for showing even the slightest interest in his gift, she removed the wrapping and let the paper fall to the desk. She stared down at a cream-colored cake of soap.

"Behold," he said, "you hold in your hand a bar of Roemermann Soap. I understand your puzzlement so allow me to explain this rather unusual gift from King Harlan to myself and now to you. Last month, when I put up overnight at a hotel in Marien-Holstein, I was promised a bar of their new and wonderful soap but through various misadventures I was forced to leave the country before receiving it.

The king evidently remembered my great disappointment and thoughtfully sent me what must be a lifetime supply."

Resisting an impulse to hurl the soap at him, she placed it none too gently on the desk. "Your gift may be unobjectionable," she said, "but your presence here is not."

"I hesitated to write or visit you," he said, "for fear I might alert Miss Gordon to our alliance."

When she made no reply, he went on. "After giving the matter considerable thought, I came to the conclusion we must lead her to believe she merely shares Prince Lothar's affections rather than having an exclusive claim on them. The prince might go to the bad, he might gamble himself into abject penury, he might pursue unwise investments or exhibit a predilection for spirits; Miss Gordon can make excuses for all of these flaws. If unable to excuse them, she can induce herself to believe her influence will eventually bring about his reformation."

Celeste stood where she was, her arms again folded. He had behaved despicably toward her, she told herself, he was a rogue and a blackguard, he was a scoundrel and worse. And yet some mischievous part of her, unacknowledged until now, admired his daring, his elan.

"Did you know," he asked, "that John Rugh, the famous Marien-Holstein philosopher, once wrote that the ideal world would be one in which all of the women were married but none of the men were? Women are aware that men tend to prefer a certain . . . what shall we say? Variety? Yes, they prefer variety in their lives but women strongly resent the fact and so punish any man who, at least to their way of thinking, transgresses in that particular way. Prince Lothar might lose his fortune gambling or become a four-bottle man and Miss Gordon will find a way to forgive him but let him merely glance at another woman and she will renounce him forthwith."

Celeste gave him a withering look. Is that how he felt, she wondered. "Do you actually believe this? About the difference between men and women?"

"As a general rule, yes I do, I find that is the way of the world. And so what I propose is to create a situation in which Miss Gordon surprises the prince in an indiscretion. With your help, of course." Without waiting for her agreement, he said, "Expect to hear from me as soon as my plans are complete."

Since as far as Rowena and the prince were concerned, her goal was the same as his, she didn't comment except to say, "Under more conventional circumstances, I trust."

His teeth flashed white in his sooty face. "One final item," he said, striding to her. Her heart leaped in mixed apprehension and anticipation. At the last moment prudence made her turn her head. Too late. His lips brushed her mouth and cheek in a tingling kiss. Before she could protest he turned away and was gone, leaving her staring after him, breathless.

Men will never understand women. If a man viewed an extremely annoyed lady with a smudge of soot on her face standing in her bed chamber while he also noted a cake of perfumed soap on the desk and a basin and a pitcher of water on a stand near the bed, the man would conclude, using irrefutable masculine logic, that the lady would most assuredly and forthwith make use of the soap and water to wash off the soot.

A woman observing the same scene, on the other hand, might very well foresee what actually *did* occur.

Celeste retrieved the soap from the desk, held it up to inhale the scent before carefully rewrapping and placing it in the top drawer of her bureau. She then sat in front of her dressing table mirror and stared wistfully at the reflection of the soot stain on her face.

Chapter 8

Roderic paused on the walkway in front of his lodgings to draw in a deep breath of the spring-like air. After consulting his watch, he decided to walk to the Admiralty. Celebrating the glorious March day, he whistled a Mozart melody as he strolled along Piccadilly, tapping his cane on the pavement in time to the cadence of the tune. Nannies gossiping on park benches smiled up at him when he passed by and he in turn nodded and touched his hat. Dogs scampered around him while children crowded onto a roundabout, small boys running as they pushed the small merry-go-round before leaping aboard and then shouting gleefully as they spun around and around and around.

Arriving in Whitehall, he stopped to admire the imposing facade of the Admiralty. How fortunate we English are, he reminded himself, to have such magnificent piles of brick and stone to house our government and our aristocracy. They bespoke sound and enduring values that made a man proud to call himself English.

Roderic was quickly ushered into the office of Mr. Algernon Thwaite. "Delighted to see you again, Lord Campion," Mr. Thwaite said after shaking hands and guiding Roderic to a seat. "You remind me more of your father with each passing year. A dedicated sportsman, your father, and an avid devotee of the turf."

When Mr. Thwaite launched into a rambling anecdote concerning Roderic's father and a race horse with the improbable name of Pot-8-Os ("Potatoes, his owner wanted to call him, or so the story goes, but the stable boy heard it as PotOOOOOOOO and put that name above the stall and thus Pot-8-Os he became"), Roderic glanced around the room, noting the leather arm chairs, the maritime instruments mounted on pedestals and the prints of ships of the line. A telescope by the window pointed in the direction of Westminster Bridge.

"I gave your epistle the most painstaking review possible," Mr. Thwaite said, "your epistle about the—the—" He frowned.

"The proposed naval treaty between England and Marien-Holstein," Roderic reminded him.

"Indeed, yes, the naval treaty. Unfortunately, Lord Howell is on an official visit to the Channel ports but Captain Trivelton has been made aware of the matter and is prepared to discuss the treaty with you. The captain is our authority on affairs concerning the Baltic Sea region."

"Marien-Holstein is on the North Sea," Roderic pointed out.

Thwaite blinked. "Of course, of course, I should

have said the Baltic and North Sea regions." He rang a miniature ship's bell on his desk and an aide appeared to escort Roderic to Captain Trivelton.

The captain, red-faced and portly, wore a black patch over his left eye. Paintings on the walls commemorated past days of glory for the British Navy: the Spanish surrender at St. Vincent, the Battle of the Nile, and Nelson's triumph at Trafalgar with an inscription beneath the picture repeating the admiral's famous signal to his fleet: "England expects that every man will do his duty."

"If only Lord Howell were in London," Captain Trivelton told Roderic. "He is, however, with the fleet."

The captain proceeded to expound on the travails of administering the navy in peacetime including the lack of prize money to encourage enlistments, the demands in Parliament for a reduction in the number of warships and the almost non-existent chance for advancement.

"The proposed naval treaty with Marien-Holstein?" Roderic asked during a lull in the captain's litany of woe.

"We at the Admiralty are most sympathetic to the treaty and to Marien-Holstein. There are, however, various legal complexities involved, namely indemnity, potential conflicts between this treaty and existing treaties with other nations, etcetera, etcetera. As a consequence, the proposed treaty was referred for review to our authority on naval law, Mr. Peter Parkinson."

Mr. Parkinson proved to be not only tall but thin to the verge of emaciation. "If only Lord Howell were with us," he told Roderic, "since the Navy Board will most assuredly hesitate to act without his presence. In his absence, I could only annotate my copy of the proposal, raising various legal points, giving citations, etcetera, etcetera, and then forward the result without a recommendation to a higher authority."

"May I speak with this higher authority?" Roderic asked.

"Certainly, Lord Campion, more than happy to oblige, come with me." He led Roderic to an inconspicuous door behind his desk and tapped on the panel.

"Come," a vaguely familiar voice called from inside.

Mr. Parkinson swung open the door and stood to one side to allow Roderic to step past him.

The man behind the desk smiled as he rose and extended his hand. "Delighted to see you again, Campion," Mr. Thwaite said . . .

A short while later Roderic walked disconsolately along St. James's Street on his way to meet Prince Lothar at White's. He no longer whistled nor did he consider the day as sublime as he had first supposed.

"Campion!"

He turned and saw Lord Appling bearing down on him. The older man grasped Roderic's arm and drew him away from the bustling throng into a quiet byway. "Are you unwell?" Lord Appling asked.

"No, yet I must confess I feel as if I just stepped off a roundabout."

"Indeed. A roundabout. Wearisome contraptions. Well. Now about the soap." Lord Appling lowered his voice to a conspiratorial whisper. "Must talk to you about that soap of yours."

Roderic put his hand to his chin. What soap? he wondered. Then, recalling his recent gift to Lady Appling, he nodded. "I daresay you mean Roemermann's Soap from Marien-Holstein."

"Precisely. Lucy is quite taken with your soap. Roemermann's Soap. Must say I am as well." He pitched his voice so low that Roderic was forced to lean toward him to hear. "I still own an interest in the Belvedere Shops. Not generally known in the *ton*. Have half a mind to stock some of your soap. What do you say?"

"Let me inform the king's chamberlain in Marien-Holstein."

"Capital. Knew I could count on you, Campion."

Lord Appling glanced furtively to right and left. "Not a word to anyone about the Belvedere Shops, Campion. Don't want the *ton* to think I'm in trade."

"My lips are sealed," Roderic declared.

With a nod and another quick look around him, Lord Appling hurried off.

Arriving at White's, Roderic settled into a chair next to Lothar and ordered a glass of madeira. Without mentioning Lord Appling, he told him about the opportunity to sell Roemermann Soap in the Belvedere Shops.

"A waste of time," Lothar said. "What do the English want with soap? They never bathe."

"Which makes this soap just the thing. If the average Englishman takes to the soap and increases his bathing from twice a year to four times the sale of soap will double overnight. And if, perchance, he decides to bathe monthly, the opportunities for the sale of soap are limitless."

"Soap! Soap! Enough of soap." Lothar threw his hands in the air. "This is no time to discuss the merchandising of Herr Roemermann's wretched soap." He patted his coat pocket. "Only this morning I received a letter from my uncle, the king, bringing both heartening and distressing news from home."

Roderic leaned forward. "The heartening news first, by all means."

"After all these years, at last the queen is with child. If she gives birth to a boy, the succession to the throne is assured; if the royal offspring is a girl, the long drought of female Reinhardts may be over at last. It goes without saying that my uncle is overjoyed."

Raising their glasses, the two friends toasted the good news. "And the distressing news from Marien-Holstein?" Roderic asked.

"The king plans to journey to London next month. When he arrives I have no doubt he intends to order me back to Marien-Holstein with the threat that if I refuse my monthly stipend will be stopped once and for all. Not so much because of my lack of success in inducing the English to sign the naval treaty but because he finds Miss Rowena Gordon an unacceptable match for a member of our royal family. Pray advise me what to do, Roderic."

"You know full well I oppose the match despite Miss Gordon's charm and beauty."

"Even so, I value your advice and counsel."

"Years ago, when I spent an inordinate amount of

time at the gaming tables, I always took followed this maxim: Walk away with a small loss before it mushrooms into an unmanageable sum. My advice to you is to break with Miss Gordon, and to do it quickly and cleanly."

"Impossible! I love Rowena with all my heart."

"Then I propose you postpone the break for a few months until your ardor cools. It will, you know, for love must wither as surely as the leaves die and fall to the ground in autumn."

"What a thoroughgoing cynic you are, Roderic. There *are* trees that don't shed their leaves, you know, and like them, my love will remain evergreen. My ardor for Rowena will never cool, not as long as I live." Lothar drained his glass and called for another bottle. "If my uncle fails to understand how determined I am, Rowena and I may be forced to consider drastic measures. We might be compelled to hurl ourselves from a cliff, locked in an embrace, to the rocks below."

Roderic shook his head, not taking the threat seriously. "That sort of thing may sound romantic, but while it might succeed in solving your immediate dilemma you wouldn't be here to enjoy your success."

"I could renounce my ties to Marien-Holstein, disavow any possible succession to the throne, marry Rowena and flee to Paris. I once dabbled with oil painting and my poems, both those in German and English, have received high praise. Is it possible that in a hundred years Wordsworth, Keats, Shelley and Byron, so much the thing today, will all be forgotten while Lothar Reinhardt is remembered?"

Roderic decided to leave the question unanswered. "Have you ever met a poet who was wealthy?" he asked. "In England we have wealthy men who create poetry but in my experience the reverse is never the case. And you must concede, Lothar, that the upkeep of your establishment requires a considerable amount of the ready."

"I admit poverty has never appealed to me, not in the least. However, Mr. Wyche's land speculation will undoubtedly bear fruit within the next few months; thereafter money will present me with no problems whatsoever."

"May I ask if your method for winning at hazard has met with success since the debacle at White's?"

"You may ask; the answer is not as yet. As you, Roderic, are well aware."

"Nor will you gain wealth through your Regent's Park land speculation since I'm convinced—nay, I'm certain—your Mr. Wyche is little better than a glib charlatan. As you will discover in the fullness of time."

Lothar held up his glass and looked at his friend over the rim. "Are you happy, Roderic?" he asked suddenly.

The unexpected question caused Roderic to pause with his glass halfway to his lips. "Define happiness," he said at last.

"Aha, you attempt to evade giving an answer. Have you ever tried to find the end of a rainbow, Roderic, have you ever chased will-o-the-wisps, have you ever taken a final fling to achieve the impossible after all rational beings despaired, have you ever done something profoundly foolish for no reason other than you wanted to?"

"Not for a very long time," Roderic admitted rather ruefully.

"I would much rather be a man who hopes for a miracle and suffers disappointment than to disbelieve as you do and be proved right." Lothar suddenly slapped the arm of his chair. "What do you think of this notion? When my uncle arrives, I introduce him to Rowena but to a Rowena disguised as a princess. Rowena will soon charm my uncle so when I reveal the deception he'll relent and insist I marry her before another day passes."

Roderic shook his head. "Miss Gordon is known to one and all. Such a scheme is doomed to fail."

Lothar sighed. "The notion *is* flawed," he conceded. "I suspect but one course is left open to me."

"And that is?"

"To await a miracle. In Greek drama, wasn't there a strange god-driven machine of some sort that tied up all the loose ends before the final curtain?"

"The *deus ex machina* it was called."

"Exactly. Be patient, Roderic, I'll have my miracle, I promise you."

Lothar, Roderic decided, had managed to coil around and around searching for a solution to his dilemma only to arrive back where he started. Both Lothar and the Admiralty seemed to have a limitless capacity for discussion rather than action. He, Roderic, was on a wearying roundabout of his own, circling and circling toward the accomplishment of his mission for King Harlan without, as yet, anything to show for his efforts.

Was there no one who could envision a goal, and

without guile, without fruitless journeys into cul de sacs and without deception, make his or her way directly toward it? His thoughts returned, as they had with surprising frequency of late, to someone who could . . .

Late that night, Celeste woke from a sleep troubled by a half-remembered dream. After tossing and turning without finding sleep again, she rose from her bed, drew a robe closely about herself and sat in front of the hearth to stare at a fire reduced to embers glowing fitfully amidst charred logs.

She crossed her arms but still she shivered. From the chill of the room? Or because this was the time of night when doubts and fears, kept at bay during the day by the sun, crept near to hover in the darkness. Old Mrs. Tremaine of the Yardley School had called this time of night the witching hours.

As Celeste's thoughts returned to her days at school, she suddenly remembered each and every detail of her dream. She had been at a ball in the assembly rooms at Guildford, a long anticipated affair, talking to two of the chaperones as she watched the dancers, all the while wishing there was someone to lead her onto the floor.

Four young men appeared in the arched doorway to the hall; one, the tallest, the most handsome and the most fashionably dressed, she recognized at once. Lord Campion. As he came to her, smiling, his two hands extended, her breath caught and the music seemed to fade.

He walked past her without a word, without a sign

of recognition, whispered in the ear of a pert miss with auburn ringlets and a daring décollètage. The young lady smiled up at him, nodded eagerly, and he led her to join the dancers whirling around the floor in a seductive waltz while Celeste watched, alone and heartbroken.

The dream had been a warning, she decided now, a warning to beware of Lord Campion. No, not of Lord Campion so much as his startling effect on her. Though she had known him for only a few weeks and they had been alone together but three times, he had come to dominate far too many of her thoughts and dreams.

Ah, but you mustn't forget, her romantic self objected, Lord Campion did drive his sleigh into the country for no other reason than to see you. And he did gain entrance to this very room to see you once again and, most convincing of all, he did take you unawares and kiss you.

Alas, how mistaken your assumptions are, her sensible self responded. The purpose of his sleigh ride over the snow was to uncover Lothar's intentions, not to see you. And his unseemly intrusion into your bed chamber was merely an escapade to provide him a story with which to regale his drinking companions at White's.

And the kiss? Did you forget his kiss?

Have you ever stopped to consider how many young ladies Lord Campion has kissed in his twenty-eight years? Are you so naive that you believe yourself to be the very first? Or so bemused to think there will never be another? Love's merely a game with gentlemen of his sort, a challenging game of hearts with a deck artfully prearranged to insure that the gentleman always wins and the lady always loses.

Yet is it possible for him to stir me as he does, for me to feel this tenderness toward him, while he feels nothing for me?

Of course it is. How are hearts broken, other than through unrequited love such as yours? Even if he entertains a certain fondness for you, doubtful though that may be, will he, a lord of the realm with his choice of any of the wealthy beauties of the *ton*, ever consider marrying you, a penniless miss from Southampton? Such an occurrence is as likely as seeing snow fall in Hyde Park in July; as likely as Prince Lothar offering for Rowena. The likelihood of either of those events occurring is less than nil.

Blinking, Celeste shook her head to dispel the last discouraging shards of her reverie. She smiled ruefully, recalling that she had been more than ready to advise Rowena to break at once with Lothar, but now, when she should take the same advice herself, she hesitated.

Banish Lord Campion from your life! she admonished herself.

And yet . . .

Crossing the room to her bureau, she opened the topmost drawer and removed the small package she had secreted there. After she unwrapped the soap, she held it up to breathe in the scent of lilacs, transporting herself from the drear winter night into the bright sunshine of springtime. And to thoughts of *him*, of Lord Campion bowing over her hand, of Lord Campion tumbling with her from the sleigh onto the snow. Her fingers touched her lips and once more she felt the tingling surprise of his kiss.

With a sigh of regret for all that could never be, she rewrapped the soap and returned it to the drawer, then walked distractedly back and forth in front of the dying fire. First she must be certain of his feelings toward her, she told herself, she must discover whether she occupied a special place in his heart or whether, as she strongly suspected, she was but one among many.

How was she to discover the truth? Not through words; Lord Campion was a man of many words, some straightforward and true but others forming embroidered designs meant merely to please. Only by his actions could she discern his true intentions.

She held still, drawing in her breath as an idea sprang full-blown into her mind. She smiled, imagining her scheme to be successful and picturing Lord Campion's surprised confusion when he learned the truth. Her smile, however, quickly changed to a frown. Her scheme was daring, perhaps so daring she would be unable to see it through to a successful conclusion; if she failed, what a sad bungle it would be. Someone else might be capable of executing the necessary ruse, but could Celeste Prescott, to whom deceit was anathema?

There was, however, no other way. She could do it, she must do it. And next week's masquerade provided the perfect opportunity, a chance that might never occur again. At the masked ball she would cleverly bring Lord Campion's true nature into the light of day. She would reveal him for what he was and in so doing dispel once and for all this strange fever that threatened to consume her.

Rowena must help her; without Rowena the plan was doomed from the beginning.

Returning to her bed, Celeste closed her eyes, determined to go forward with her plan no matter what the risks might be. Tomorrow, she told herself as she drifted into sleep, tomorrow she'd ask for Rowena's help.

Chapter 9

When their carriage became caught in the crush of vehicles bringing revellers to the masquerade, Roderic and Prince Lothar walked the final quarter mile to Darlington House, Roderic in the garb of a highwayman with a pistol thrust through the scarlet sash at his waist and a slitted black scarf across his eyes, Lothar resplendent in the turban and flowing robes of a Turkish sultan.

"I distinctly recall," Lothar said as they waited to surrender their invitations, "that you always professed to detest masquerades."

"With good reason. Later tonight, when the gentlemen and the ladies remove their masks, do you realize what will be revealed beneath? No? Let me tell you then. We'll see other masks, the ones they don on waking and wear thereafter. Since the life of the *ton* is already a masquerade, one more always seemed rather superfluous to me."

Lothar shook his head. "I honestly believe I

understand why you insist on viewing life from your cynic's perch—from which you look down on the rest of us mere mortals. The reason is simplicity itself, although I'd be willing to wager almost any sum you'll deny it."

"You have a wager."

"The reason is that you, Roderic, have never been in love."

"That, my friend, is complete and utter nonsense." He smiled in fond remembrance. "Why, I've been in love dozens of times."

"Thus proving my contention," Lothar said with a decisive nod. "Any man who claims to have been in love dozens of times has never really been in love at all. What he calls love is an emotion of an entirely different ilk."

Roderic started to answer, then shrugged. What was the use of debating the point? Lothar, smitten as he was with Rowena, evidently believed everyone should suffer from a similar affliction. He, Roderic, was having none of that! Let Lothar see life through the rosy haze of love if he wished; he would see it as it was, clearly, warts and all.

And yet, strange to tell, he looked forward to tonight's masquerade, despite the impression he might have given Lothar. In his years of self-imposed exile, he told himself, he must have missed the excitement of London more than he thought. He missed the bustle and the challenge of the ever-changing city, the give and take of wit around the dinner table, the beauty of the women.

After surrendering their invitations in the reception room, they walked along a hallway leading to the ballrooms, Lothar pausing now and again to exclaim over the beauty of the many-colored lights sparkling in the orange and rose trees. To Roderic the display seemed grotesque, as though the Vauxhall Gardens had been uprooted, placed in pots and carted indoors.

When they paused at the top of the stairs leading to the first of two large rooms, Roderic looked to his right and saw that a performance was under way. My God, he thought as the appreciative crowd applaused, another rope dancer and another juggler. Would London never tire of rope dancers and jugglers?

The other end of the room had been curtained off. To the martial call of a bugle, the curtain was drawn aside and the partygoers, abandoning the rope dancer and juggler, surged toward the small stage to watch redcoats and Highlanders firing their muskets at an unseen enemy. In the center of the scene, a general raised his sword, his signal sending his troops forward with the redcoats wielding their bayonets, the Highlanders their swords.

The general staggered, clutching his breast. The red of blood seeped through his fingers and he fell. Roderic felt a shiver of recognition when officers, a tattooed Indian and a soldier with a furled flag gathered around their fallen leader and the scene became a *tableau vivant*, a living picture duplicating Benjamin West's painting "Death of Wolfe," celebrating the English victory over the French at Quebec in 1759.

"Bravo!" someone shouted and the call was taken up in a chorus of cheers.

Lothar touched Roderic's arm as they started down the stairs. "I see Rowena with her mother," he said. "There, on the far side of the room near the doors to the balcony."

With quickening interest Roderic followed the direction of his friend's nod, at first recognizing only Mrs. Gordon, attired in French baroque style with a canary yellow gown whose hoops made her, he estimated with an uncharacteristic lack of gallantry, as wide as a park bench. Marie Antoinette? he wondered. Above her domino mask her powdered hair had been pulled to an astounding height, enabling it to encircle a small cage containing a live canary swinging on his perch.

When Roderic drew nearer he saw Rowena at her mother's side with her face and arms darkened, looking tiny and defenseless in a beaded buckskin dress and moccasins. Her long black hair was braided and adorned with a single white father. As Roderic carefully scanned the masked faces nearby, he felt a twinge of disappointment. At the moment at least, the Gordons, mother and daughter, appeared to be alone.

They made a strange pair, Roderic thought, Marie Antoinette and Pocahontas, the glittering queen of France and the pagan princess of America. He knew that Mrs. Gordon was perfectly capable of fending for herself and so needed no help from him, but for the first time, he felt a stirring of sympathy for Rowena's plight. Did she see herself as a stranger in a strange land, much as an American Indian maiden might after being brought to London to be exhibited to swarming crowds of the curious?

After introducing him to Mrs. Gordon, Lothar glanced around the room before looking significantly at Roderic and then remarking to Rowena, "I fail to see your delightful companion. Is Miss Prescott about?"

Rowena shook her head. "Unfortunately a severe attack of the megrims kept her confined to the house. Alas; she so wanted to attend a masquerade."

"What a shame," Roderic said in his most offhand manner. "I looked forward to seeing her again."

As the talk swirled about him, Roderic withdrew into a communion with himself. What he had said was true and yet at the same time quite false since it represented a deliberate understatement. He was, he realized with a shock, devastated by Celeste's failure to appear at the masquerade. The anticipation he had felt earlier had dissipated with news of her illness and he was left quite forlorn. Yes, that was the only word for his condition. Forlorn.

How had he come to this? he asked himself. This behaving like a green country lad would not do, it would not do at all. Hadn't his mission for Marien-Holstein put enough on his plate as it was? Miss Celeste Prescott was a nobody from Southampton who possessed neither wealth nor social position. Though admittedly atttractive, she could not be called a great beauty. Come to think of it, he wasn't certain he even liked the young lady. How could he possibly be when their acquaintance was limited to three rather brief meetings?

He had been too long away from England and from London, a city he both loved and hated. That was the only reasonable explanation for his state of mind. After months in foreign climes the first reasonably presentable English miss to appear had caught him unawares. Exactly. He smiled to himself: now that he had diagnosed the cause of his malady, he was able to assume the role of apothecary and prescribe the cure.

As he had told Lothar, in his youth he had been in love dozens of times. Marianne had dazzled him with her beauty in June only to be superseded by the witty Clarissa in July who, in turn, was replaced by Georgiana—what a lovely singing voice Georgiana had—in August.

He had no need to ask where those and other delightful young ladies were now; he knew. For the most part they were married and were the proud mothers of bouncing boys and girls. And yet there were always other charming and talented Mariannes, Clarissas and Georgianas for him to fall in love with, each London season brought them forth in abundance. And almost all of them must be coming to tonight's gala masquerade. The young woman who could cure him of this ridiculous beguilement might very well be entering the room at this very moment.

He looked over the heads of the throng to the entrance stairway. A few minutes before the Wolfe tableau had been reenacted and smoke from the firearms was now drifting across the steps, obscuring his view. As the smoke cleared, Roderic drew in his breath and stared. Magic! he murmured. He had wished for someone to appear and lo! She had.

She stood at the top of the stairs dressed all in white except for a single red rose in her hair. As Roderic looked more closely he realized she wasn't wearing a gown but was enwrapped in white veils, veils that concealed her face as well as swathing her body to just above her ankles, veils that demurely revealed her enticing curves while at the same time hinting that she wore absolutely nothing else. As she started down the steps, the sudden flash of pale skin told him the veils had been draped in such a way that when she walked her shapely right leg was daringly revealed half way up her thigh.

Not another Marianne nor a Clarissa nor a Georgianna, he told himself with an appreciative smile, but a creature even more delectable—Salome and her seven veils. She was the very medicine he required.

Celeste followed Mrs. Campbell, a still-young widow who had been sworn to secrecy, to the top of the steps leading down to the ballroom. Biting her lip, she hesitated as smoke from a tableau drifted in front of her. The wildly beating wings of butterflies fluttered in her stomach.

You have naught to fear, she tried to assure herself. No one can possibly recognize you as the missish Celeste Prescott, not in the black wig and outrageously risqué Salome costume with seven veils artfully arranged with tucks and ties requiring not a single pin to preserve your modesty. You *are* Salome, not Celeste, and so you must behave as you imagine Salome behaved. Lord Campion can't possibly pierce your disguise and so you must do all in your power to make up to him, and in so doing force him to reveal his true character, show him to be either sincere or nothing more than a trifler.

When the smoke cleared she started down the steps, trying to ignore the stares of the gentlemen below her, her head held high despite her acute awareness that the drape of her chiffon veils caused each step she took to reveal an indecorous view of that unmentionable part of her, her leg.

Since she intended to play the flirt with Lord Campion—she wondered if she knew how to go about it—her first challenge was to find and be introduced to that gentleman. She was turning to Mrs. Campbell to ask whether her companion espied him anywhere in the crush below when, to her heart-stopping surprise she saw a highwayman striding toward the stairway, toward her.

Despite the costume, a broad-brimmed hat, a many-caped coat open to reveal a long-barreled pistol secured by the red sash at his waist, and black riding boots, she had recognized Lord Campion at once. He was all in black except for the red sash just as she was all in white except for the red rose. They were dressed as opposites as, of course, they actually were.

He swept off his hat and bowed low to her. "May I have the honor of this dance?" he asked.

She glanced at the lissome Mrs. Campbell in her

guise of Robin Hood, unsure how or if she should respond, but received no help. No wonder masquerades were considered rather daring, Celeste thought. They required no introductions. A young lady's only defense against a predatory gentleman was her right of refusal.

She certainly wasn't about to refuse. Hadn't she come here for this very purpose? Inclining her head, she accepted Roderic's proffered arm and let him lead her into the second room where, almost as if awaiting their arrival, the band struck up a lively country tune and she was whirled from partner to partner.

"I must have been mistaken," Roderic said when next they came together.

Had he thought he recognized her at first? Is that why he asked her to dance? "Mistaken?" she asked, pitching her voice to a low huskiness to avoid detection.

Before he could reply, the dance separated them.

"When I glimpsed you through the smoke at the top of the staircase," he said when he again took her hand, "I told myself it was impossible for you to be as lovely as I thought. As I say, I was mistaken. Now that I see you face to face, veil or no, I realize you are as lovely as I imagined, if not more so."

Tears sprang to Celeste's eyes as they parted. Lord Campion had repeated, almost word for word, the compliment he had paid her when first they met. How foolish of her to have treasured his words these many days. How naive. Now, crestfallen, she perceived them not as glittering jewels but as the dross they were.

Her vision blurring, she stumbled slightly. When dabbing at her eyes failed to stem the tears, she turned from a startled partner and fled from the floor, entering the first room she came to and closing the door behind her. Finding herself alone, she crossed the room to lean on a small stand as she drew in deep breaths to quell her agitation.

When the tears stopped she looked around, finding herself in a book-lined room lighted by French globe lamps suspended from the high ceiling. The coverings of the many ottomans placed at random on the floor matched the pale green satin and white silver muslin of the draperies. Glancing down, she found her hands resting on a book on the stand, a book open to a richly detailed depiction of a scene in an Eastern palace where houris in diaphanous pantaloons with partially exposed breasts reclined languorously on enormous red and green pillows. She stared at the picture, both shocked and fascinated.

Hearing the sound of the music swell as though the door behind her had been opened, she hastily shut the book and turned to find Lord Campion watching her. He closed the door and slowly walked toward her as she tried to still the rapid beating of her heart.

Stopping a few feet away, he asked, "Was I at fault in some way?"

"I felt light-headed," she said to avoid answering his question.

She had behaved like a goose, Celeste told herself, since the compliments a gentleman of the *ton* might lavish on a lady at their first meeting gave little evidence of his real character. No matter how disappointed she might be to have to lower the value of his praises since discovering he bestowed them indiscriminately, she still had not solved her quandary, had not achieved her goal of proving him true or false. Weeping would accomplish nothing. She vowed to be bold, not tearful.

"Are you fully recovered?" he asked.

She nodded, afraid to speak more than necessary for fear he would recognize her voice.

He smiled as his gaze lingered on her costume. "Since I see no unnatural curvatures, I realize you can't possibly be carrying a vinaigrette. Is there something I could bring you? A glass of champagne perhaps?"

She shook her head.

"I was hoping against hope you might dance for me."

"Do you mean with you?"

"No, I hoped I could persuade you to dance *for* me, as Salomé once danced for Herod. I thought you might imagine me to be Herod, a Herod already enchanted by you but willing to be even more enthralled by your dancing."

When he reached to her she held her breath, transfixed by his nearness. Lifting the end of one of her filmy veils, he said, "I hoped you might perform the dance of the seven veils. Not for the multitude"—he gestured toward the ballroom behind him—"but for me alone."

Hoping the veil covering her face concealed her vivid flush, Celeste stepped to him until she was only a whisper away. Taking the veil from him, her fingers stroking his hand as she did, she looked up into his eyes. "And if I danced for you," she asked, "what would you, a highwayman, offer me in return?"

"Like Herod, I offer you any gift that is in my power to grant." His eyes, glowing warmly through the slits in his black silk scarf, unsettled her. "Name your boon. Ask for anything at all."

A kiss. Unbidden, the wish flicked into her mind before she could rein in her runaway imaginings. What was she thinking? Sincerity and honesty and constancy, she reminded herself, were what she really wanted from him. But Salomé could hardly ask for those.

Trying to break the spell woven by his nearness, she stepped back, forcing her gaze from his. "You have a pistol," she said in a teasing voice, reaching out and touching the weapon thrust through the sash at his waist. "I expect you could use your weapon to compel a lady to do whatever you might wish."

He shook his head. "Never would I resort to such tactics," he said. Easing his fingers under her veil, he caressed the side of her face, sending tingling shocks coursing through her. "I much prefer persuasion." As he gently stroked her cheek, her breath caught and, all unconscious of what she was doing, she ran her fingers back and forth along the barrel of his pistol.

His touch traced a fiery path from her cheek to her lips, where he slowly outlined the curves of her mouth. As her pulses raced, her mouth opened slightly and she felt the tip of his forefinger on her tongue. Impulsively, she kissed his finger. Horrified by what she'd done, Celeste gasped and drew back; for a moment they faced one another as time stood still.

With a cry of confusion, Celeste turned and started to flee from him only to have his hand grasp one of her veils. She felt the veil pull away, baring her shoulders. When shelves of books blocked her way, she stopped, standing with her back to him, hearing nothing but the wild pounding of her heart.

She sensed him approaching her from behind. Suddenly his arms encircled her waist and he drew her back toward him, pressing her body to his. Despite her shock of pleasure, she gripped his wrists, intending to force him to release her but failing to carry through her intent. She found herself stroking his hands instead. Murmuring endearments, his lips trailed kisses along her bare shoulder, pausing at the nape of her neck as she trembled with an inexplicable yearning that rendered her helpless.

Slowly he turned her to face him, all the while keeping her in the circle of his arms. His gaze flicked downward and she heard his sharp intake of breath when he saw the rise of her breasts above the wispy chiffon veil. Looking up into her eyes, he gently lifted the edge of the veil concealing her face until her mouth was uncovered, then his lips sought and found hers.

How warm his lips were, so warm and tender, encouraging her to respond. Unable to resist, she snuggled closer as her own lips parted under his. He groaned, his grasp tightening around her body as now he kissed her with a smoldering passion that scorched through her, setting her aflame. Forgetting why she was here, forgetting everything, her arms twined around his neck to hold him to her, to keep him forever hers.

"Salomé," he breathed, his lips still against hers. "Salomé," he murmured again.

The alien name pierced her like a dagger of ice, shocking to her senses. She was not Salomé, she was Celeste. His words weren't meant for her, they were intended for someone else, his lips didn't kiss her, they kissed the stranger he thought she was.

He had betrayed her.

She broke free and fled from the room, stifling a cry that bespoke a grievously wounded heart.

Chapter 10

At the Darlington House masquerade, the many-tiered chandeliers burn brightly above the glittering assemblage. If you journey east to Charing Cross, however, you will find a darker, lonelier city where the streets and walkways are empty except for an occasional carriage that rumbles into view, clatters past and disappears into the gloom. If you could look through one of the few lighted windows along the street, you would be more likely to view a scene from mundane lives rather than witness the fashionable world at play.

This is no place to dawdle in the early hours of the morning so you hasten northeast from Charing Cross along The Strand for about a quarter of a mile, turn right toward the River Thames on Adam Street and walk for one short block, turn right again, this time onto John Street, proceeding a hundred or so feet to the third house on the right and you will have arrived at the present abode of Mr. Samuel Wyche.

Mr. Wyche owns this small, undistinguished brick house, living on the first floor while renting out the ground and third floors. Mr. Wyche, who makes a habit of frequently changing his place of residence, has a methodology for selecting houses just as he has a methodology for discovering bargains in vacant land; namely, searching for a house that is markedly inferior to all of those in its immediate vicinity. His house on John Street easily passes this test.

Mr. Wyche's flat is at the top of a narrow, unlit flight of stairs. Notice the neatly lettered card on his door: "Mr. Samuel Wyche, Bookseller." Over the years, Mr. Wyche has pursued many occupations, some honorable, many less than honorable, but at present his energies, which are considerable, are directed to only two, namely speculation in vacant land and the non-publishing of books.

While a summary of Mr. Wyche's literary activities has little relevance to Lord Campion, Celeste Prescott, Prince Lothar and Rowena Gordon, such a description will succinctly illustrate at least one less than admirable facet of his character.

Mr. Samuel Wyche, Bookseller, specializes in the memoirs of members or former members of the demi monde. He purchases their vivid accounts of various scandalous liaisons with the young blades of the *ton*, many of whom, by the time the memoirs are written, have matured into responsible members of the aristocracy. Mr. Wyche then generously promises to withhold publication if the gentlemen will but submit payment to Mr. Wyche for valuable services rendered. The fact that Mr. Wyche, to date, has actually published only one three-volume book shows that very few of these gentlemen have refused his offer.

Entering Mr. Wyche's bachelor flat on this, the night of the masquerade, we find him seated in a high-backed chair industriously penning a letter. One candle burns steadily on his desk but for reasons of economy there is no other illumination in the shadowed room.

Although a dancer of more than average ability, Mr. Wyche did not seek an invitation to the masquerade. In fact, he dislikes dancing, learning only to assist his pursuit, many years ago, of a certain Mrs. Elizabeth Hornbeck, a wealthy and, as it turned out, all-too-impressionable widow.

Don't be misled by this incident, however, for women were not and are not of particular interest to Mr. Wyche; his one passion is the relentless pursuit of money. Strangely, once obtained, the money is of little interest to him. Then again, perhaps this is not so strange, considering the many gentlemen, almost all of whom would consider themselves Mr. Wyche's betters, have a passion for pursuing foxes but little interest in the fox itself. (Consider, if you will, how few times, if ever, one finds sauteed fox served at a country squire's dinner.)

John Rugh, the Marien-Holstein philosopher, touched on this very point in his justly-renowned *Treatise Number Three* when he wrote that in the best of all possible worlds men would search for their Holy Grails but none would ever find them.

How on this dark night is Mr. Wyche attempting to satisfy his passion for the accumulation of money? Draw closer and look over Mr. Wyche's

The Publishers of Zebra Books
Make This Special Offer
to Zebra Romance Readers...

AFTER YOU HAVE READ THIS
BOOK WE'D LIKE TO SEND YOU
4 MORE FOR *FREE*
AN $18.00 VALUE

NO OBLIGATION!

ONLY ZEBRA HISTORICAL ROMANCES
"BURN WITH THE FIRE OF HISTORY"
(SEE INSIDE FOR MONEY SAVING DETAILS.)

shoulder. Perhaps this letter—it appears to be directed to an associate in business—will provide us with a clue:

"... and the moneys received from P.L. total seven thousand five hundred pounds for half interest in 'The Wyche London Land Company'. Expenditures to date have totaled one hundred and seven pounds, eight shillings, and six pence as itemized in the attached accounting. After deducting my commission (in the amount of ten percent, as agreed) I will personally deliver the remaining moneys to you within the next fortnight.

"You may rest assured that the above mentioned P.L. entertains no suspicions whatsoever concerning the legitimacy of our enterprise. In fact, if the sum mentioned above were not the total of his available funds, he would willingly, nay, eagerly, advance a considerably greater amount.

"I will apprise you within the next few days of the location of my new lodgings since under the circumstances I must remove myself from these quarters in the very near future.

"Your most faithful servant, S.W."

But wait, this is no ordinary business letter. It reads more like a message from one conspirator to another. Who is this confederate, the mastermind behind what appears to be a plot with "P.L." its hapless victim? Unfortunately, the first page of the letter is turned upside down so we must bide our time and hope Mr. Wyche in some way reveals his associate's identity.

Have a care, step back into the shadows, for Mr. Wyche is rising from his chair. He yawns, he stretches. Now he begins his preparations to retire for the night. Soon he will snuff the single candle leaving us, alas, to await another day for the answer to our question.

Chapter 11

After a supper served at one in the morning followed by several more hours of dancing, the masquerade at Darlington House came to an exhausted conclusion at dawn. Celeste, who had slept but fitfully after arriving home before midnight, heard the whispered voices of the returning revellers before dozing off to sleep until noon.

By the time she was up and about her despair had turned to anger. At first, Lord Campion and his duplicity bore the brunt of her fury, but since he was not at hand, her anger soon came to focus on Mrs. Gordon, who was.

Her employer had been, after all, the cause of her distress. Jane Gordon had, by misrepresenting herself as a respectable matron when she was in fact nothing of the sort, induced Celeste to accept the position of chaperone to her daughter. If she had not become Rowena's companion she would never have met Lord Campion.

In one of the inner recesses of her mind, Celeste

realized she was perhaps being unduly harsh in judging Mrs. Gordon. Yet she brushed this nagging doubt aside. Mrs. Gordon had lied to her and she meant to confront her with that fact before her employer left the house to return to Brighton.

She approached Mrs. Gordon later that same afternoon. "I must speak with you," she said.

Mrs. Gordon seemed about to agree, but after observing Celeste closely, shook her head and said, "No, no, no, no, not now. After our musical evening."

"Our musical evening?" This was the first Celeste had heard of it.

"Tomorrow night I plan to entertain a small group of friends. All very impromptu, of course. You, my dear, will play the pianoforte. I recall how extravagantly your references praised your skill, and Rowena will sing, she has a lovely though untrained voice, and my sister, Jessamine Cathcart, has agreed to favor us with selections played on the harp. The *piece de resistance* will be Mr. Robert North, who has promised to read his latest poem accompanied by a musical counterpoint. Provided by myself."

"I was under the impression you intended to return to Brighton today."

"I did so intend, my dear, I most certainly did, but events change plans just as much as plans alter events and so I postponed my departure until two days hence. A mother must make sacrifices for her only daughter." She lowered her voice. "Confidentially, and by that I mean you must not breathe a word to Rowena, not one single word, I have a surprise in store for her at our musical evening."

Celeste, with no notion as to what Mrs. Gordon might have in mind, waited with the expectation all would soon be revealed—as it was, at least in part.

"While at the masquerade, I was informed that Prince Lothar meant to journey to Portsmouth for a visit lasting several days. I made it a point not to discover his reason for departing town since the less I know about that particular gentleman, the better. Taking advantage of his absence, I invited a gentleman of the *ton* to my musical evening, a gentleman I suspect may very well win Rowena's heart."

"From my observation, that appears unlikely. Rowena truly believes herself to be in love with the prince."

"Of course she does. Today she loves this prince from that hyphenated kingdom of his, tomorrow, God willing, she will find she loves another. Someone, I trust, who will win her heart at our musicale." Putting her forefinger to her chin, Mrs. Gordon frowned in thought for a moment before saying, "Perhaps you could play a Haydn sonata. I've always been partial to Haydn. I find him so much more civilized than Mozart. So much more English."

Celeste had never been convinced that she possessed more than a modicum of musical talent. "I really think I should be excused from playing, Mrs. Gordon," she said. "More months than I care to count have passed since I last practiced, and even then my playing, I fear, was less than accomplished."

"All the more reason you should devote your time between now and tomorrow practicing while I spend mine making the arrangements." And with that Mrs. Gordon turned away and was gone, leaving Celeste with little choice but to practice lest she make a complete muddle of the Haydn.

The next evening Celeste decided to wear her new willow green percale gown that had a hem scalloped to reveal a lace edged petticoat; both hem and the vee of her decolletage were decorated with artificial red roses.

As soon as she was dressed, she hurried down the stairs to the drawing room to practice the Haydn sonata a few more times before Mrs. Gordon's guests began to arrive. She had scarcely opened the piano and started to play when she sensed someone enter the room behind her. Thinking it must be Rowena, she went on playing.

"Lovely," a man's voice said. "With a bit more practice you could become an accomplished pianist."

She stopped abruptly and looked over her shoulder to find Lord Campion standing behind her holding a small box wrapped in white and tied with a red ribbon. Recalling their last meeting at the masquerade, she quickly averted her head to conceal the color rising to her face. How in character for him to introduce himself by complimenting her playing. He was like a gambler who placed random wagers in the hope one would win at long odds. She caught herself up short; how cynical she had become. That was one of Campion's traits, not hers.

In an attempt to quell the turmoil his unexpected arrival created in her—she had assumed he had left town with Prince Lothar—she resumed playing only to strike a succession of wrong notes. With a sigh of exasperation, she gave it up.

She refused to let him unsettle her like this!

"I hope your health has improved," he said.

What could he be referring to? Of course, her excuse for her supposed absence from the masquerade. "I feel quite well," she told him.

Nodding, he placed the beribboned box on the pianoforte and sat on the bench beside her. She edged away, tempted to rise and flee but unwilling to allow his unsettling presence to drive her from the piano.

"My father," he said as he started to play, "who had the honor of meeting Haydn when the composer was a guest of the Duke of York at Oatlands in the early '90's, always maintained that Haydn had a slightly faster tempo in mind. Something more like this."

She listened in surprise as his fingers danced over the keys. How well he played! Reluctantly she had to agree that his interpretation of the sonata far surpassed hers, but she refused to give him the satisfaction of telling him so. She would be perfectly civil to him, she decided, no more and no less.

He ended the piece with a flourish of his own devising and then, still sitting beside her, reached to retrieve the box. "I brought this gift for you," he said, offering it to her.

"I have no need for any more soap," she told him tartly.

His lips twitched in amusement. Not at her reply, she suspected, but at some secret of his own. "This is not soap, I swear to you," he said. "Here, hold the box, you'll find it light as a feather."

Though curious, Celeste shook her head, rejecting the gift. "I think not," she said.

He raised his eyebrows, started to speak but then shrugged. "Did you know Lothar won't be here tonight?" he asked.

Wondering what new tack Lord Campion was about to take, she nodded.

"He was forced to travel to Portsmouth," Campion said. "Since his uncle, King Harlan, arrives in London next week, Lothar must do all in his power to encourage the Admiralty to sign the naval treaty." After glancing behind them as though suspecting eavesdroppers, he lowered his voice. "My plans for trapping Lothar in an indiscretion are almost complete," he confided. "I discovered the means to that end at the masquerade even though I left early in the evening. When I discovered your absence, the affair held little charm or meaning for me."

How deceitful you are, Lord Campion, she told herself bitterly. You stayed long enough to make love to a stranger. At least you thought she was a stranger.

"I noticed that Lothar paid considerable attention to a saucy miss," he went on, "a raven-haired young lady disguised as a gypsy girl. When I made inquiries the next day, I found her to be a certain Mrs. Jeanne Atkinson who is not only a widow who makes her home in Duke's Row in Somers Town but also a young lady who is no better than she should be. I intend to drive out to Somers Town to meet Mrs. Atkinson and I have every reason to believe she will be more than willing to cooperate if I offer her an appropriate incentive. I assume you will assist me when the time comes to spring my trap."

Celeste hesitated. It was true she had agreed to cooperate in Lord Campion's plans but her promise had been given before the masquerade. More importantly, of late she had been having doubts about the wisdom of interfering in Rowena's life, doomed though her friend's love for the prince might be.

"As soon as my arrangements are complete," he went on, "I intend to—" At that moment he was interrupted by a woman's voice calling his name.

"Ah, so there you are," Mrs. Gordon said, sweeping into the drawing room. "So glad you could come to my little party, Lord Campion."

He rose to his feet, at the same time awkwardly reaching behind him to place his gift on top of the pianoforte, fearful, or so Celeste supposed, that Mrs. Gordon would think it was meant for her. As Lord Campion bowed over his hostess's hand, Mrs. Gordon looked past him to favor Celeste with a nod and a knowing smile.

At first Celeste failed to understand her meaning. And then she brought her hand to her mouth to hide her gasp. Could it be, she asked herself, that Lord Campion was the mysterious gentleman of the *ton* designed to wean Rowena's affections from the prince? Hearing Mrs. Gordon begin to praise her daughter in the most extravagant terms, she decided he must be.

Mrs. Gordon's ploy was doomed to failure, she assured herself, for Lord Campion would never so basely betray his friend, the prince. Or would he? Now that she had discovered the depths of his deceit at the masquerade, she realized there was no limit to how far he might go to accomplish his ends.

No matter what Lord Campion did or did not do, Rowena would most certainly spurn his blandishments. Or would she? She had on more than one occasion, Celeste recalled, expressed admiration for Lord Campion and now, with the prince absent, she might be at least temporarily entranced by Campion's attention and compliments.

Whatever the outcome of Mrs. Gordon's stratagem might be, she, Celeste, was in no danger of being wounded. Her interest in Campion had ended at the masquerade; since then she had taken pains to erect what amounted to a wall of glass between the two of them.

Before she could find out more about Mrs. Gordon's plans, Harkins began announcing the arriving guests. Rowena appeared shortly thereafter looking, Celeste thought, as perfect as a picture in a gown of dotted Swiss with hem and neckline delightfully trimmed with an appliqué of green satin leaves.

When Lord Campion greeted her with a bow and a few murmured words, a vivid flush suffused Rowena's cheeks. Celeste, though telling herself she was indifferent to what passed between them, was still disappointed not to have been able to overhear his words.

Rowena, she soon discovered, had still another admirer at the musical evening. Mr. Hugh B. Garson, one of the last to arrive, paid scant attention to the other guests as his gaze followed Rowena wherever she went. Mr. Garson, Celeste recalled, had unsuccessfully offered for Rowena the year before.

"I like Hubie as a friend," Rowena had told her, "but only as a friend. Besides, he has a great partiality for dogs."

"Is that so strange?" Celeste wanted to know. "I like dogs myself."

"As I do. Hubie Garson, though, has more than fifty of them, which is quite too much of a good thing. He takes them everywhere with him. I suspect that at this moment he has several waiting for him in his carriage."

Though he had not, Celeste noted as he took a seat, brought one with him into the Gordon town house.

Chairs had been carried into the drawing room where they were arranged in five rows with four or five to a row. Since Mrs. Gordon had decreed that the music would come first with the refreshments served afterwards, all of the guests were soon seated and the entertainment commenced.

Ill at ease, Celeste took her seat on the piano bench and began playing the sonata, surprised to find herself using Lord Campion's quickened tempo. At first all went well and she had started to relax when she happened to glance up and saw his beribboned gift still sitting where he had placed it atop the pianoforte. Her concentration wavered and she grimaced to hear the discordant result. Drawing in a determined breath, she recovered at once and succeeded in completing the piece without further mishap. With a sigh of relief, she acknowledged the modest applause and returned to her seat in the last row.

After Mrs. Gordon's sister, Jessamine, played several selections on the harp, Rowena left her place beside Lord Campion and walked to the front of the room to sing a Scottish air accompanied on the piano by her mother.

As Rowena sang in a clear though untutored soprano, Celeste glanced toward Lord Campion sitting at the far end of the row in front of her. She found him gazing admiringly at Rowena, smiling as he nodded in time to the music. Celeste, after assuring herself that she felt nothing, no jealousy, no bitterness, no despair, absolutely nothing at all, looked quickly away.

Following Rowena's encore, Mrs. Gordon introduced the honored guest of the evening, a man who, she avowed, was all the rage at the moment, the young poet Mr. Robert North. Mr. North, his mop of curly brown hair bobbing over his garret-pale face, bowed in acknowledgement when greeted by warm applause.

"I will read my latest poem," he said, "a modest effort dedicated to romantics not only here but everywhere, a poem entitled 'An Ode To Love.' Mrs. Gordon"—he bowed to his hostess—"has most graciously offered to accompany me on the pianoforte."

He raised his head slightly, cleared his throat, then

closed his eyes as he began to recite:

> "All ideas, all hopes, all joys,
> Whate'er moves our mortal frames,
> All are harbingers of Love,
> Who 'nounce his sacred flames."

As the poet paused at the conclusion of the stanza, Mrs. Gordon at the pianoforte supplied what sounded to Celeste like a valiant though not completely successful attempt to reproduce a series of bird calls.

"'Nounce?" Celeste heard Lord Campion, taking advantage of the clamor of the birds, whisper to Rowena, "I know not 'nounce."

As the bird calls ended, Mr. North went on declaiming his ode, pausing after each stanza for Mrs. Gordon to add her musical interpretation of his words. When he finished the twenty-eighth and final stanza, the audience applauded with enthusiasm. It was impossible for Celeste to determine whether they were saluting the felicity of his poetry, Mrs. Gordon's musical accompaniment or the cessation of both.

"After listening to your applause," Mrs. Gordon said as the poet returned to his seat, "I feel certain you will all agree with me when I say that the lyrical masterpieces of Mr. Robert North will be honored after the poems of Lord Byron are forgotten."

"But," Celeste heard Lord Campion murmur, "surely not before then."

Despite her coldness toward him, she found his comment so apt she was forced to suppress a smile.

The evening's entertainment having concluded, the company repaired to the dining room for a light supper of roast duck, leg of lamb, fried carp, artichoke bottoms, cauliflower, tarts and various other meats, fish, vegetables and desserts.

Celeste sat across from Robert North who immediately became the center of the most flattering attention. Though she tried to remain attuned to what he was saying, she found herself glancing toward the far end of the table where Lord Campion was expertly carving a duck and solicitously placing thin slices on Rowena's plate.

As she watched, he paused in his carving and, with the carving knife pointed at Robert North, said, "I congratulate you on an extraordinary performance, sir; such an unusual combination of the muses of poetry and music."

North smiled in a self-satisfied way. He must think Campion is praising him, Celeste told herself. She was none too certain that was the case.

"In the arts we must always be prepared to experiment," North said, "whether in poetry, music or painting. Even, Lord Campion, when the attempts fail to live up to our expectations."

Ah, thought Celeste, good for you. Perhaps Mr. North would be able to hold his own with the overweening Lord Campion after all.

"We live in a new age, my lord," North went on, "requiring new approaches. While we see the many faults of our society, I suspect those who come after us, our posterity, will look back on this as the very best of times. As Mr. Wordsworth wrote, 'Bliss was it in that dawn to be alive, But to be young was very heaven!' "

"I admire your optimism," Campion said with evident sincerity, "and your good judgement in choosing to write of such a universal emotion as love. Who hasn't experienced love in one form or another, yet who among us can adequately define it?"

"Just so, sir," North agreed. "Perhaps St. Paul gave us a clue when he wrote that 'Love beareth all things, believeth all things, hopeth all things, endureth all things. Love never faileth.' "

"But what is love?" Campion persisted.

To Celeste's surprise, Mr. Hugh B. Garson, who had been exceedingly quiet all evening, was the first to answer. "To my way of thinking," he said, "loyalty and faithfulness are the truest expressions of love. Traits rarely found in humans."

"To me," Mrs. Gordon said, "love should be an adventure. An exploration." She glanced around the table as though seeking approval for her notion. "Yes, a lover is akin to a dauntless explorer. When one is young, one's map of life is most dreadfully empty with huge portions labeled *'Terra Incognita.'* When you love you explore those unknown regions, you discover that some are as beautiful as our English countryside in the spring of the year; others as desolate as any American wilderness."

"Bravo!" Mr. North cried. "You, Mrs. Gordon, are the one who should have been the poet rather than myself."

Mrs. Gordon beamed.

After several of the other guests had given their

conceptions of love, Mr. North turned to the far end of the table. "I notice that you, Lord Campion, have remained strangely silent even though you were the one who propounded the question."

Celeste looked at Lord Campion, expecting his definition of love, if he deigned to attempt one at all, to be a facile quotation from a poet or a masculine echo of Mrs. Gordon. His reply surprised her.

"I hesitated to speak for a very good reason," Lord Campion said. "At one time, when I was younger, I thought I understood what love was and pursued it as best I could. Alas, I found I was mistaken. Therefore, I can only admit to profound ignorance, Mr. North. In truth, I know not what love is. Perhaps I raised the question in the hope of finding a clue to the answer."

"Fair enough, sir," North said, "since the attainment of knowledge must begin with an admission of ignorance." He looked directly across the table. "And you, Miss Prescott, how do you view love?"

Disconcerted by the attention, she shook her head but, after the silence lengthened, she said slowly, "Love is two people who become as one. Two people who learn to trust and respect one another, who are honest with one another and, of course, faithful in their love. Each must put the good of the other above his or her own good."

"How charming to hear such idealism in such a jaded city as ours," Mr. North commented.

"Unfortunately, people can never abide the ideal. They praise it in the abstract but reject it when it occurs." Celeste glanced along the table, realizing to her surprise that the speaker was Rowena.

"When they see love," Rowena went on, "true love, they do all in their power to thwart it. Perhaps from envy." She lowered her head and said no more.

As another guest offered his definition, Celeste saw Lord Campion lean toward Rowena and whisper a few words in her ear. Rowena smiled wanly and, reaching to him, covered his hand with hers. Celeste quickly looked away but not before she felt a twinge of pain. She had observed that women who had been disappointed in love, as Rowena most certainly had, often sought solace from the first sympathetic gentleman to appear.

Lord Campion, she thought bitterly, was sympathetic. He was also, in matters if love, without a conscience.

Chapter 12

"Miss Prescott," Mrs. Gordon said, "did you wish to speak with me?"

The supper was over, the last of the guests had said their good-byes only moments before and Celeste and Rowena were on their way to the stairs leading to their bed chambers.

Celeste nodded, turned to clasp Rowena's hand as she murmured "Good-night," and then followed Mrs. Gordon into the drawing room.

The row of chairs and the harp were gone so the room looked as it had before the musicale. With one exception: the small box wrapped in white and tied with a red ribbon still sat on top of the pianoforte. The sight of Lord Campion's gift brought back all of Celeste's despair, causing a wave of misery and hopelessness to sweep over her. She blinked her eyes to hold back her tears.

Mrs. Gordon rang for Harkins. "Will you join me in a glass of sherry?" she asked.

Celeste started to decline only to change her mind

almost at once and nod.

After sitting across from Celeste in a chair near the hearth, Mrs. Gordon glanced up at the portrait of her father, the general, over the mantle. Celeste had noted that whenever her employer entered this room, her gaze invariably gravitated to the painting. "He would have hated every minute of it," Mrs. Gordon said.

"The musical evening?"

"Exactly. The general always claimed to be tone deaf and used that as an excuse to avoid attending musical events of any sort. I never knew him to sit through an opera and he absolutely detested amateur musicales."

Looking up at the General's stern countenance, Celeste remembered the first time she had been in this room, the day she met Mrs. Gordon. Recalling how the other woman had beguiled her into becoming Rowena's companion, her anger rose. And yet, now that she was face to face with the older woman, she hesitated to accuse her of deceit.

Celeste took two generous swallows of her wine in an effort to bolster her flagging courage. One of Mrs. Yardley's favorite maxims came to mind: *"Fortes fortuna juvat."* She agreed, fortune did favor the brave.

"You give every appearance of being vexed and testy," Mrs. Gordon observed, "as you have ever since I returned from Brighton. Have you found my daughter less amiable than I promised?"

"Not in the least. As far as Rowena is concerned, I have nothing of which to complain; in fact I consider her my friend. I find her even more gentle and charming than I had any right to expect."

"Do you intend then to tell me you despair of showing her the folly of her attachment to the prince?"

"I find myself wondering whether it *is* folly, whether she may well be right in listening to her heart while all the rest of us are wrong in opposing her. When I heard tonight that the prince was in Portsmouth to attempt to sway the Admiralty to sign the naval treaty, my first inclination was to wish him well."

"The naval treaty?" Mrs. Gordon seemed surprised. "What naval treaty might that be?"

Celeste told her of the prince's mission on behalf of Marien-Holstein and the difficulties he was having in rousing the British to action.

"I avoid news of the prince like the plague," Mrs. Gordon admitted. "While charming in the eyes of some, Lothar, unlike Lord Campion, is weak in so many ways. I could never abide a weak man."

There was some truth in Mrs. Gordon's criticism of the prince, Celeste admitted to herself. And yet "weak" did Lothar less than justice. "What fails to please you," she protested, "might very well satisfy Rowena. And evidently does."

"Am I to understand you asked to speak to me tonight to support the prince's claims? If so, you waste my time and yours as well."

Celeste drank the last of her sherry. Drawing in a deep breath, she said all in a rush, "Not at all. I wished to speak not of the prince, not of Rowena but about yourself. You were less than honest with me when first we met. You misled me, you deceived me about the nature of your visit to Brighton, and much more, besides."

"Ah, I understand," Mrs. Gordon said with a weary sigh. Putting down her glass, she leaned forward. "Does Rowena know? About—" She hesitated. "About Brighton and so forth?"

"Not through any words of mine, but yes, she does know the truth. And has for many, many years."

Mrs. Gordon sank back into her chair, her body slumping, her face sagging. Suddenly she looked much older than her forty-some years. In the harsh light from the fire, Celeste saw how overly rouged her cheeks were and noted a dark tear-trail in the corner of one eye left by the cosmetic she used to darken her lashes. Despite herself, she felt a pang of sympathy for Mrs. Gordon.

"Ah, well, so be it then," Mrs. Gordon said. "I must talk to her," she murmured more to herself than to Celeste, "and I will come morning." Rallying, she sat up straighter and fixed her gaze on Celeste. "I never lied to you, Miss Prescott," she said. "I may have omitted certain facts, facts that were no concern of yours at the time and are no concern of yours now, but I never lied."

"You deceived me," Celeste persisted. "You had no right to deceive me."

For a moment she thought the older woman meant to contradict her but she did not and the silence lengthened. "When I married Mr. Richmond," Mrs. Gordon finally said, "I was all of sixteen years of age."

Richmond? It took a moment for Celeste to recall that after her husband's death her employer had "recaptured" her maiden name.

Mrs. Gordon shook her head in wonderment, as if what she was about to say never ceased to amaze her. "I imagine I was much like you are now, a wide-eyed, eager young lady who naively believed in love everlasting. Marriage to Mr. Richmond changed all that. Marriage awakened me to what life was really like."

"I've never seen a picture of Mr. Richmond," Celeste said, unable to think of any other response.

"For a very good reason. I never want either myself or my daughter to be reminded of him." Her voice rose in anger. "Never." She went on in a softer tone. "Rowena was born at the end of my first year of marriage and then the following year I lost a baby girl. My physician warned me never to think of having more children if I valued my life."

"I'm so sorry," Celeste murmured.

"As I was at the time. My mother had eight children, all still living, praise be to God. Believing, as she did, that women were created to have children, I looked on myself as having failed in my marital duty. As did Mr. Richmond, who made no attempt to conceal his feelings."

Celeste's sympathy for Mrs. Gordon increased. "How terrible. A husband should always support his wife but especially during times of distress and sorrow."

"Men are more interested in the birthing of male heirs than in what they consider feminine moodiness. At least my Mr. Richmond proved to be. He turned his back on me and our marriage deteriorated into a mere pretense. His affairs of the heart became notorious in the *ton* but if I so much as glanced at a man over the edge of my fan he flew into a terrible rage that lasted for days on end."

Celeste sought to mute her growing sympathy by reminding herself that she was hearing but one side of the story. If Mr. Richmond had lived, his depiction of these events would undoubtedly be much different. There must be at least two versions of all marriages, even happy ones, she told herself, each at variance to the other.

"I owe Mr. Richmond a great debt, however," Mrs. Gordon said. "He taught me what the great majority of our so-called gentlemen of the *ton* are like once you manage to penetrate their chivalric facades."

Thinking of Lord Campion's betrayal, Celeste had to admit that there was at least some truth to what Mrs. Gordon said. At the same time, her sense of fairness forced her to protest. "You paint with too broad a brush," she objected. "Prince Lothar, for one, may have more than his share of faults, yet I suspect he means well."

"You damn with faint praise. Weak men often do mean well but I, for one, find them both dull and exasperating. For all his shortcomings, Mr. Richmond was never dull." She smiled in remembrance but almost at once shook her head and the smile vanished. "Mr. Richmond fancied himself a Nimrod, a nonesuch shooter and hunter. I hate to recall how many tiresome hours I was forced to spend at the dinner table listening to him regale his guests with tales of his feats in field and wood. Most of them, myself included, were bored to tears."

Celeste frowned, unable to understand what Mrs.

Gordon was trying to tell her.

"One of those hunting tales of his taught me a valuable lesson about men," Mrs. Gordon said. "In it he described at great length how he rose before daybreak, left his hunting lodge at dawn and, after he was in the woods for less than ten minutes, saw a magnificent stag. Lo and behold, instead of turning tail and leaping away the deer actually approached Mr. Richmond, as though accustomed to men and therefore not afraid of them."

"And so naturally your husband spared the deer's life."

"Not at all, my dear Celeste, he killed him with his first shot. Did Mr. Richmond then consider himself a wondrous success and retire from the hunt for the rest of the day? Of course not. *Au contraire*, he complained of the ease of the kill and proceeded to seek a more elusive quarry, a more worthy opponent. When I heard his tale of that particular hunt, I understood all I needed to know of men. Or just about all."

"You found out about men because of the way your husband hunted deer? I fear I fail to grasp your point."

"Think of it this way. We, the females of the species, are the deer. Women are the prey. To gentlemen of the *ton*, the courtship of women is a sport exactly as hunting is. Merely another sport, neither more nor less important to them except for the hope of perpetuating themselves through their male offspring. Those heirs are akin to the deer heads mounted on the walls of their hunting lodges."

Celeste frowned. How cynical, she thought, how terribly bitter Mrs. Gordon was. And how sad to think of anyone feeling this way.

"I was unfortunate enough to be the deer Mr. Richmond killed at the very start of his hunt." Mrs. Gordon gradually grew more animated. "Don't you see, I should have mistrusted him during our courtship, should have feared him, yet I never did. I may even have encouraged him, been the slightest bit forward. And so he married me just as he shot and killed that deer, and then I failed him or so he thought. And what did he do then? He left me behind to go on with his hunt. And came to consider the most elusive of his prey to be the most attractive, those women who flirted with him, who teased him by flattering him one moment and pretending to flee from him the next."

"How predatory you make men seem," Celeste said, shaking he head as she shuddered with distaste at the notion. On the other hand, wasn't Lord Campion exactly that? "In your view, have men no sense of honor? No sincerity? No human kindness?"

"Certainly they do, a few of them. Many other men want to possess all those traits but have forgotten how. They need a woman with the ability to bring their more admirable qualities to the fore. As I have done for several men since Mr. Richmond passed on to his reward. My secret is simplicity itself. No matter what inducements a gentleman offers, I refuse to marry him. Once married, a man's sport ceases since his goal is attained. Refuse their offers of marriage, maintain your independence, and their pursuit waxes rather than wanes. At least until desire fades."

"Surely love lasts, at least true love must be everlasting."

"Everlasting love." Mrs. Gordon smiled. "Ah, my dear Celeste, how young you are! Perhaps one love in a thousand endures. All others quickly lose their luster. The time arrives when anticipation is replaced by apathy, when the footfall once eagerly welcomed is heard with a shrug of indifference. Alas and alack, if one is married when this occurs, escape is well nigh impossible."

Celeste bit her lip. "I could never believe as you do, Mrs. Gordon."

"Not now, perhaps; now you believe as I once did. Wait twenty years, nay, wait but ten and then think back on what I said tonight. I warrant you'll have changed your tune."

"Never! Not in ten years or twenty years or thirty years."

"I suspect I know the reason for your vehemence. And also the reason for your anger toward me, for they appear to be one and the same." Mrs. Gordon smiled. Wistfully? Tenderly? "My dear, you fancy yourself to be in love."

"In love? No, not I, not in the least. Who could you possibly imagine me to be in love with?"

Without a moment's hesitation, Mrs. Gordon said, "Lord Campion."

Despite herself, Celeste blushed.

"Your vivid flush confirms my suspicions."

"I may have reddened but you misconstrue the reason. Only a few days ago he showed himself to be unworthy of my love or of anyone's love. Lord Campion proved himself to be a deceiver and worse. I redden from anger, not affection."

"Anger? No, the cause lies elsewhere. When I

watched you tonight while Rowena sang and later at the supper table, I saw how your gaze returned to him again and again. Never have I witnessed a young lady more in the throes of the tender passion."

In her eagerness to make Mrs. Gordon understand how impossible it was that she could have the slightest tender regard for Lord Campion, Celeste lost her customary reserve. "How could I be, knowing how fickle Lord Campion is?" she asked. "Tonight he lavished his attentions on Rowena while at the masquerade he made love to me thinking I was a stranger disguised as Salomé. How can he pretend he cares for me in the slightest when at my first absence he betrays me."

"Whether you happen to be the object of Lord Campion's affections is another matter entirely. Have you ever stopped to consider that he may have made love to Salomé because he wants to deny the great tenderness he feels for you? In matters of love, I find that men are cowards more often than than the heroes of myth or legend."

Celeste stared at Mrs. Gordon, appalled at having revealed so much. At the same time, hope stirred in her breast. The thought that Lord Campion might be perturbed by his feelings for her had never entered her mind. She dismissed the idea almost immediately. "No, impossible, not Lord Campion."

"And you feel no affection toward him?"

"None, not after the masquerade. Perhaps at first I did, he does possess a certain charm, a grace, a manner. Something. But no, I have no tenderness for him, not in the least, not at—" She felt her throat tighten as though her conscience sought to prevent her from telling any more untruths.

Celeste drew in a tremulous breath and lowered her head. "What you say is true," she admitted in a whisper. "I do care for Lord Campion more than I have for any other man, ever before. Or ever will again." She choked back a sob, closing her eyes while she tried to calm herself. To no avail. "And there's nothing I can do about it," she said, "nothing at all."

Mrs. Gordon came to her, putting a comforting hand on her shoulder. Mrs. Gordon, Celeste told herself, was no longer her employer nor her deceiver, she was another woman who showed compassion. Celeste rested her cheek on the older woman's hand and for a time neither spoke.

Mrs. Gordon broke the silence. "I understand," she said softly. "I'm so sorry. But there's no shame in how you feel. Or in admitting it."

Celeste turned to look at her. "What can I do? What can I possibly do?"

"How can I answer that question? When Lord Campion marries, and I suspect he will eventually, he'll choose someone of his own kind. If it were someone else, someone suitable for you, I'd say you must follow your heart, Celeste, no matter where it leads you. I'd advise you to seize the chance for love since it may never come again. But Lord Campion?" She shook her head.

Celeste pondered her words. Unsuitable? She had turned from Lord Campion because he had betrayed her, not because she deemed herself unsuitable. She, Celeste Prescott, was every bit as good as any man, Lord Campion included. She had believed this ever since she was a young girl and she believed it even more ardently now.

If Lord Campion hadn't deceived her, would she have dared to follow Mrs. Gordon's advice and obey the yearning of her heart? There was no way she could tell. All of the strictures remembered from her childhood argued against it and yet something warned her not to be too certain. Never before had she felt as she had when Lord Campion kissed her. And wasn't half a loaf better than no bread at all?

She roused from her reverie with an inconsistency in Mrs. Gordon's reasoning nagging at her. "What of Rowena?" she asked. "You advise me to risk all for love. Would you tell your daughter to do the same?"

Mrs. Gordon said, "Apples and oranges, apples and oranges! The two situations are simply not the same." She turned away from Celeste and walked to the pianoforte, picking up the ribboned box, idly examining it and then putting it down again. "Besides being weak, the prince is betrothed to another," she said.

"Everyone agrees the betrothal is an arranged engagement not of the prince's choosing. If his family has a change of mind, shouldn't Rowena have a chance to follow the dictates of her heart?"

"That would be a different matter entirely," Mrs. Gordon said coolly. She put her hand to her forehead and rubbed her temple. "This has been a horribly long day for me," she said, "and I believe I feel a fit of the dismals coming on. And I must leave for Brighton on the morrow."

Celeste, suddenly feeling exhausted herself, rose slowly from her chair. "You were right about the reason for my upset," she admitted. "It was wrong of me to lash out at you the way I did." She raised her hands and let them fall to her sides in a gesture of hopelessness.

Mrs. Gordon came to her and embraced her. "Good night," she said. "Sleep well." As she started to leave the room she paused and then walked to the pianoforte. "Someone must have forgotten this," she said as she again picked up Lord Campion's gift.

Celeste held out her hands. "Yes, I did. The box is mine."

Mrs. Gordon raised questioning eyebrows but when Celeste offered no explanation she shrugged slightly, handed her the box and again walked to the doorway. "Good night," she said once more.

"I wish you a pleasant journey to Brighton tomorrow," Celeste said.

Holding Lord Campion's gift in both hands, she climbed the stairs to her bed chamber where she placed the box on her desk. After using a taper to light the lamp, she stood looking down at the box. When she claimed it in the drawing room, she had intended to leave it unopened. Now, though, curiosity plagued her. What could Campion's gift be. She was tempted to change her mind.

No, she would not! Come morning she would put the box away in the deepest recess of her wardrobe and forget about it just as she meant to forget about him. She wanted nothing from Lord Campion, nothing at all.

But, as she changed into her nightgown, her gaze returned again and again to the bright red bow and when she went to the desk to extinguish the lamp she hesitated with her hand extended, staring at the neatly wrapped and brightly beribboned box, more and more tempted to at least look inside.

Lord Campion will never know if I opened his gift or not, she assured herself. Quickly undoing the bow, she laid the ribbon to one side and removed the white paper, at the same time breathing in the spicy scent of sandalwood. Opening the lid of the ornamented box, she reached inside and drew forth her gift.

She stared down at the gauzy strip of white chiffon in her hands, her heart racing when she realized she held the veil she'd left behind at the masquerade. Lord Campion had returned it to her. So he had known all along that she was Salomé! He had made love to her, not to a stranger. Holding the chiffon to her breast, she smiled radiantly.

He hadn't betrayed her after all.

Chapter 13

Returning to his rooms after dining at Watier's as the guest of Lord Appling, Roderic glanced through the cards and letters that Dumas, his manservant, had left for him on the silver tray on the table in the entry, noting with disappointment that once again there was no message from Celeste. He had expected her to write thanking him for the return of her veil. Could it be that she had never opened the sandalwood box? No, that was highly unlikely, since every women he had ever known had possessed an insatiable curiosity.

Why, then, the silence?

Nor had he received a letter from the Continent. He shrugged away this second disappointment, telling himself he would most certainly have an answer to his urgent inquiries before many more days had passed.

After pouring himself a glass of madeira, he settled in a commodious arm-chair in the room he referred to as the library because his landlord had left behind, on one of the otherwise bare book shelves, the complete eight-volume set of Gibbon's *Decline and*

Fall of the Roman Empire. There was no evidence that any of the volumes had ever been opened.

Very soon, Roderic told himself with a fleeting smile, he would be qualified to write a shorter, more personal work: *The History of the Decline and Fall of the Prince Lothar-Rowena Gordon Alliance.* Or would *Misalliance* be more appropriate? One volume consisting of five chapters should suffice, the first chapter recounting the origins of the ill-fated romantic alliance together with his justification for thwarting it, followed by chapters detailing each of his three main initiatives, The Campion London Plan, The Campion Somers Town Plan and The Campion Continental Plan, the book concluding with a modestly phrased description of the final triumph of his well-planned, well-executed campaign.

Already his London Plan was far advanced, awaiting only the opportune moment to bring it to fruition. His equally ambitious Continental Plan held great promise but awaited an answer to his letter to Stuttgart. As for Somers Town, he meant to drive there early tomorrow to enlist the cooperation of Mrs. Jeanne Atkinson.

The unsigned naval treaty remained a burr under his saddle for he had failed to gain the attention of the Admiralty just as surely as Prince Lothar had failed. The prince had recently returned from his journey to the south of England a discouraged man. Though he had succeeded in tracking the elusive Lord Howell to a seaside estate near Worthing, his discussion with that gentleman had proved as brief as it was unrewarding.

"Lord Howell is approaching his allotted three-score-and ten years," Lothar reported, "and unfortunately his memory comes and goes. For some reason unknown to myself, he evinced great interest in the masquerade at Darlington House, inquiring as to the names of the guests, who accompanied whom and so forth and so on. As for the treaty, I suspect he'd never heard of it before I brought it to his attention and I know for a fact he has absolutely no desire to hear of it or of Marien-Holstein again."

With luck, Roderic assured himself, something would eventually turn up to save the treaty, hopefully before next week when King Harlan arrived in London. He, Roderic, had let fly a great many arrows aimed in as many directions as possible; one certainly would strike a target somewhere before long.

His main concern now, though, was Mrs. Jeanne Atkinson of Duke's Row, Somers Town, the no-better-than-she-should-be widow . . .

Shortly after noon on the following day, he drove his hired curricle north through Bloomsbury to Somers Town, exulting both in his expectations of success and the mild March weather. Somers Town, a district as much country as city and neither fashionable nor disreputable, boasted (or, as some would have it, suffered from) a large colony of French emigrés.

Inquiring after Mrs. Atkinson at the local alehouse, Roderic received directions accompanied by a knowing Gallic wink. Minutes later his knock on the door of the modest semi-detached house on Duke's Row was answered by a tall black servant wearing a red turban who ushered him into the parlor. At his entrance, the two young women sitting on a sofa near the hearth looked up expectantly from their tea.

Recognizing the prettier of the two as the dark, brown-eyed gypsy fortune teller from the masquerade, he bowed and started to introduce himself.

"Fanny," said Jeanne Atkinson to her companion, "will you be so kind as to inform this gentleman of the error his ways?"

"Most certainly I shall," said Fanny. Turning to Roderic, she said, "Mrs. Atkinson, being an exceedingly proper lady, never deigns to speak to a gentleman prior to being introduced."

"I was attempting to introduce myself."

"No," said Fanny, "that won't do, not at all. A third party is required. Only last week at the opera Lord Alvanly entered Jeanne's box and sought to speak to her without an introduction and she cut him dead. Never in my life have I seen a gentleman so disconcerted."

"Here then." Roderic handed Fanny a sealed letter. "Pray present this to your friend and ask her if it will suffice."

Accepting the letter, Jeanne opened and read it. "Pray inform Lord Campion," she said to Fanny, "that I accept the introduction provided by Lord Appling."

Fanny smiled up at Roderic as she relayed her friend's message. "You rode with Appling in the Park last summer," said Fanny to Jeanne. "He was the older gentleman who sells scents and salves."

"Yes," said Jeanne, "I rode with Lord Appling but no, his father sold the scents and salves. Owned the Belvedere Shops, he did, and God knows what else.

Appling's wife thinks him too grand to be in trade. But Lord Campion isn't here to discuss Appling."

"Appling or his father," answered Fanny, "it's all of a piece to my way of thinking. I never cared above half for gentlemen in trade. Except for my Mr. Mitchell. You do recall my Mr. Mitchell?"

"The cotton merchant from Edinburgh?" asked Jeanne.

"The very one. Made me laugh, he did, with his clever witticisms and his *bon mots*. 'You must stay up late at night thinking of them,' said I, 'they're all such hits, such palpable hits.' 'Never,' said he, 'why should I spend my nights thinking of hits when I could just as well be amusing myself with misses?' I never laughed so much in all my life as when I was with Mr. Mitchell, cotton merchant or not."

Jeanne tapped an impatient toe on the floor. "You were on your way to Sophie's, I believe," said she. "Pray give her my love."

Fanny opened her mouth as though to protest, then glanced up at Roderic. "Oh, yes, how forgetful I am," said she with a conspirator's knowing smile. Rising, she kissed her friend good bye and rewarded Roderic with a smiling nod. *"Adieu, adieu,"* she called back from the doorway.

Had he once found bits of muslin such as Jeanne and Fanny amusing? Roderic wondered. He supposed he had, many years ago. Admit it, he'd found them not only amusing but vivacious and entertaining, saucy and tempting as well. And now? The truth was that featherheads no longer held his interest. He preferred a woman with more depth of mind, someone, in fact, very like Celeste Prescott.

Jeanne was extending her hand to him; Roderic blinked and, returning to the present, bowed and kissed it, at the same time inhaling the too-heady fragrance of her lavender scent.

"Oh, my," said Jeanne, rising to her feet, "I fear your cravat's awry." She stood exceedingly close to him to adjust the bow. When he glanced down his gaze was drawn to the dark valley between her breasts revealed by the provocative cut of her mulberry afternoon dress.

"I drove here to beg a favor," Roderic told her.

"I thought as much."

He told her in considerable detail what he wanted from her.

For a moment Jeanne stared at him in surprised silence. "Prince Lothar, the gentleman who wore a sultan's robes at the masquerade? You want me to urgently request him to come to me tomorrow evening and in return you agree to give me forty pounds, twenty now and twenty after I succeed." She looked up at him coquettishly from under her long lashes. "Is that *all* you want from me, my lord?"

"Make certain he remains with you for at least an hour. Which should pose no problem for such a charming young lady as yourself."

The fingers of her right hand deftly undid the top button of his waistcoat, then moved lower to linger at the next. "None at all," she told him.

"Excellent."

She undid the second button.

Not particularly tempted while at the same time somewhat confused because he was not, Roderic stepped back and started to leave.

"Wait," said Jeanne. Walking to one side of the room, she tugged on a bell-pull. When her turbanned servant appeared, she said, "Show Lord Campion to the door."

As he left the room, Roderic heard her giggle and then laugh aloud. He drove away wondering if she found his precipitous flight amusing or whether something else entirely had inspired her laughter.

Later that day Celeste received a lengthy letter from Lord Campion. Her eager anticipation faded to disappointment when she read his impersonal message describing his plan to have Rowena discover Prince Lothar committing an unforgivable indiscretion and telling her how she could assist him. He closed by reminding Celeste of her pledge to be his partner in the undertaking.

How could she have agreed to be a party to such a shameful deception, she asked herself. Even before she finished reading the letter, she knew she would refuse to help Campion. Rowena must be allowed to follow the promptings of her heart no matter how hopeless the outcome might appear to be; any woman should have such a chance. She, Celeste, deserved no less herself.

Her inclination was to write Lord Campion at once to explain her decision and plead with him to abandon his plan. No, she believed in honesty so first she must now be completely honest with Rowena, tell her what she and Campion intended and plead for her forgiveness.

She found Rowena in her bed chamber reading a

novel. Impulsively, she knelt on the rug beside her friend's chair and described Campion's scheme to lead the prince into an indiscretion. "I have no excuse for what we meant to do," she said when she finished, "none at all. I deserve your condemnation and whatever punishment you may want to mete out to me."

Rowena, who had listened to her tale in stunned silence, put aside her book and took Celeste's hands in hers. "How was I to learn of the prince's meeting with this woman?" she asked.

"Lord Campion intends to send an anonymous letter to alert me to the prince's rendezvous on Duke's Row in Somers Town. I was to encourage you to drive to the trysting place at the designated hour to observe at first hand the prince's impropriety. How sordid it all sounds now. How could Campion have induced me to help him?"

"Somers Town," Rowena repeated thoughtfully. "A tryst with a young lady the prince supposedly admired at the masquerade. Do you happen to know her name?"

"A Mrs. Atkinson. Jeannine? No, Jeanne. Mrs. Jeanne Atkinson. A widow, I believe."

"Ah, of course. The saucy gypsy fortune teller with a penchant for adjusting men's cravats. At the masquerade she read the prince's palm and informed him that she saw love and happiness in his future. She neglected to say he would find it in Somers Town."

"Are you acquainted with this Mrs. Atkinson?"

"She *is* rather notorious." Rowena lowered her voice. "For two years and more Lord Radley is said to have given her two hundred a month as well as the use of his horses and carriages. That, of course, was before Miss Ackroyd caught Lord Radley's eye."

Celeste, though taken aback by Rowena's knowledge of the amorous escapades of the *ton,* said nothing.

"Do you expect Lord Campion to be at the scene of this supposed rendezvous?" Rowena asked.

"His letter gives no hint." Celeste paused. "Knowing Lord Campion, however, I suspect he will be there, hoping to observe the confrontation and then to savor his success."

"I agree." Rowena smiled as if savoring a secret triumph of her own.

"He so prides himself on his cleverness," Celeste said, recalling his gift of the veil in the sandalwood box.

How he must have enjoyed making her believe he had betrayed her! How he must have relished the notion of revealing the truth by means of his gift! Without giving a moment's thought to the anguish he had caused her in the interim.

"You intend to write Campion?" Rowena asked.

"Without delay, to tell him I want no part of his underhanded scheme. To let him know that you trust the prince implicitly and so have no intention of appearing in Somers Town tomorrow evening or at any other time."

"I have a different idea," Rowena said slowly. "Send no answer to Campion, let him believe you intend to fall in with his plans. Tomorrow night both you and I will drive to Somers Town and observe whether Lothar keeps his rendezvous with

Mrs. Atkinson."

Celeste, having never intended the plan to proceed, was aghast. Evidently she had erred in confessing to Rowena. What if Lothar did appear in Somers Town? What then? Did Rowena have so much confidence in the faithfulness of her prince that she could never imagine him being tempted by another woman? If so, she was more naive than Celeste had thought possible.

"You must let me write Campion," Celeste pleaded.

"Absolutely not. Promise me you won't communicate with him in any way before our journey to Somers Town. If you have any regard for our friendship, you must promise."

What choice did she have? "I give you my word," Celeste said reluctantly, all the while fearing that disaster awaited Rowena on Duke's Row . . .

The anonymous letter arrived the next afternoon giving the time of the prince's rendezvous as nine that evening and providing precise directions for finding the house on Duke's Row. Shortly after eight, Harkins drove Rowena and Celeste north in the Gordon's closed carriage along roads narrowed by piles of earth where wooden water pipes were being replaced by the new cast iron ones.

They arrived well before nine, stopped a short distance from the Atkinson house on the opposite side of the street and extinguished their lamps. Though the March days were mild—Celeste had seen crocuses and wallflowers in bloom—the night still held a cool reminder of winter. Rowena and Celeste drew shawls close around their shoulders as they settled in to wait.

A light glowed from a front ground floor window of the Atkinson house but they saw no carriages or other signs of visitors.

"We shall catch cold for naught," Celeste said. "The prince isn't here nor will he come."

"Only time will tell," Rowena responded with what, to Celeste, seemed undue complacency.

"We should never have come here. Lord Campion is certain to have used trickery of some sort to lure the prince to Somers Town."

"In matters of this sort," Rowena said, "the important thing is not so much whether the gentleman appears but what occurs shortly thereafter."

Celeste shivered, again feeling a premonition of an impending tragedy that would devastate Rowena. And all because of Lord Campion. How utterly different they were, Celeste thought, she and Campion. He thrived on deception while she detested it. He attempted to win by means of devious stratagems while she believed in honesty. How foolish of her to waste her thoughts on someone so different, so unsuitable, so unattainable.

For she did think of him often; no, more than often. In fact she seldom thought of anyone or anything else, even though she remained unaware of his intentions regarding her. He had recognized her at the masquerade and so she couldn't accuse him of betraying her. But what he had not done proved nothing about what he meant to do.

She closed her eyes, feeling an ache of longing as she remembered him coming up behind her, his arms circling her waist to draw her back against him, remembered the delicious tingle of his lips kissing first her bare shoulders, then her cheeks, then her lips.

No! Shaking her head, she opened her eyes to banish Lord Campion from her thoughts once and for all. As though she could! The bittersweet memory of his kisses, she realized with a heartfelt sigh, would be with her for the rest of her life . . .

Rowena suddenly tensed, grasped Celeste's hand and leaned forward. A horse's hoofs pounded on the dirt road behind them and a phaeton clattered past. It was, however, too dark to recognize the driver or to tell whether there was a passenger at his side. They waited expectantly. Was the phaeton slowing as it neared the Atkinson house?

A man's voice shouted in French from the phaeton, another answered, and both burst into the chorus of a what sounded like a drinking song. The singing faded as the phaeton drove on until it finally turned and disappeared from their view. Rowena sank back against the cushions, releasing Celeste's hand.

"We should leave," Celeste said, "since, as you can see, the prince has no intention of coming tonight."

She felt Rowena stubbornly cross her arms. "The prince," she said, "is usually tardy when he visits me so I have no reason to believe he'll be any more punctual this evening."

How calm Rowena seemed. Or was she being fatalistic, determined to accept whatever the evening had in store for her?

"Did you know," Rowena asked, "that Mr. Hugh B. Garson, known to his friends as Hubie, offered for me during my come out season?"

What a strange comment for Rowena to make at a time such as this, Celeste thought. After all these months, could her friend have abandoned hope and started considering her other chances for marriage? She could think of no other reasonable explanation.

"So you mother told me," Celeste said, "and I was introduced to Mr. Garson at the musicale. I found him a most pleasant young man."

"My mother favored his suit," Rowena said without emotion, "and I genuinely liked Hubie. I might well have accepted him if it were not for those horrible dogs of his, especially when ten of them are Irish Wolfhounds. I like dogs, but fifty are too many. Of course I was young then and had yet to meet Prince Lothar."

As she spoke the prince's name another carriage—to Celeste it looked like the curricle the prince usually drove—approached from behind them, slowed as it went by and stopped in front of the Atkinson house. The driver leaped to the ground, tethered his horse at the post and sauntered up the walk. As he neared the door he was briefly silhouetted against the lighted window.

Celeste gasped. "Prince Lothar," she murmured, glancing at Rowena. Her friend sat staring intently at the prince as he knocked at the door and was admitted without delay.

"What do you intend to do?" she asked Rowena.

"At the moment, nothing. We must be patient, we must bide our time."

Celeste shook her head but made no reply. *This is my doing,* she reminded herself, *I should never have told Rowena about Campion's plan. Perhaps at times like this it's best to be slightly less than honest.*

The minutes dragged by as they continued to watch the Atkinson house. After what seemed an eternity to Celeste but was probably, she admitted to herself, no more than five minutes, a moving light appeared at an upper window as though someone walked across the room holding a candle. The shadows thrown by the light steadied as if the candle had been placed on a table. Suddenly the window darkened.

And still Rowena waited.

At last she summoned Harkins, who opened the carriage door and handed Rowena and then Celeste down to the walkway at the side of the road. While fearing what they would discover, Celeste at the same time felt a relief to be up and doing.

"Miss Gordon, do you wish me to—" Harkins began.

"Remain here," Rowena told him.

They followed the walkway until they were opposite the Atkinson house where Rowena paused before leading the way across the street. This is madness, Celeste told herself, but she remained silent for she could think of nothing she could do or say that would deter her friend.

Without hesitation, Rowena walked to the front door and, instead of knocking, lifted the latch, opened the door and stepped inside. Standing on tiptoe to look over Rowena's shoulder, Celeste saw a small entry hall with stairs to her right climbing upward into darkness and, directly ahead, an archway leading into a lighted room. Rowena walked swiftly beneath the arch with Celeste a step behind.

A pretty dark-haired woman in a lavender gown with a low scoop neckline looked round-eyed at them from where she sat, alone, on a sofa. Seated across from her, Prince Lothar's hand was poised in midair. In his hand was a teacup.

Prince Lothar placed his cup on a saucer on the table beside him, leaped to his feet and strode to Rowena, clasping both of her hands in his and bringing them to his lips while Celeste stared at them in surprise.

Rowena stepped away and said, "I do believe Campion lurks nearby."

Lothar crossed the room, nodding to Celeste as he brushed by her, threw open the front door and called "Roderic!" There was no reply. Again he shouted, "Roderic!"

After a few seconds a puzzled-looking Roderic appeared. Lothar ushered him into the parlor with a bow and a sweep of his arm. Roderic's gaze lingered for a moment on Celeste before he looked around the room. He frowned, glancing at Lothar and then at Rowena for an explanation.

Rowena walked to him. "How nice to see you once again, Lord Campion," she said coolly. "I don't believe I had the opportunity at the masquerade to introduce you to Mrs. Jeanne Atkinson. I expect you know that Mrs. Atkinson is my aunt," she said with a malicious smile. "Or do you?"

Chapter 14

Roderic stared at Jeanne Atkinson. Celeste had never seen him so taken aback.

"You never informed me of your relationship to Miss Gordon," he accused the widow.

"Fancy that!" said Jeanne "May I be so bold as to remind you, my lord, that you never troubled yourself to ask?" She smiled sweetly up at him. "May I also remind you, my lord, of your debt of twenty pounds. A bargain is, after all, a bargain, and since I fulfilled my part of—"

Roderic raised his hand to silence her. "You need have no fear," he said stiffly. "You shall receive your pieces of silver."

"She's not the betrayer, not the Judas," Lothar told him. "You, after all, were the one who attempted to hoax both Rowena and myself."

Celeste was surprised to find the prince seemingly more saddened and hurt than in a high dudgeon at his friend's perfidy. In his place she would have been furious.

"You plotted behind my back," Lothar went on, "and your scheme failed. How frightfully unlike you, Roderic. You not only betrayed me, you did it ineptly."

Roderic extended his arms sideways with his fingers splayed in a gesture of surrender and, perhaps, of admission of guilt and apology for his actions.

Celeste smiled with satisfaction. How marvelous to see Lord Campion humbled! And yet she couldn't help feeling sorry for him, this proud man brought low, humbled in front of his friends by Jeanne Atkinson. How very human he appeared in this moment of defeat.

"Celeste," Rowena whispered, "I have no wish to remain in the same room as Campion; he offends my every feeling. Let me show you Aunt Jeanne's garden before I say more to him than I should."

Rowena opened a door near the ingle-side and led the way into a walled enclosure where flagstone paths radiated from a central sun dial. The garden lay in shadow but a glow above the neighboring rooftops gave promise that the moon would soon rise.

"In summer the garden is lovely," Rowena said. "Aunt Jeanne spends hours every day tending her roses, hollyhocks and geraniums."

Celeste refused to allow herself to be diverted. "I was so worried when we drove here, not knowing what to expect, never suspecting that Mrs. Atkinson was your aunt. You should have told me the how and about of it all."

"Yes," Rowena said softly, "I don't know why I didn't."

"I deserved my heartache," Celeste admitted. "I should never have agreed to abet Lord Campion in his ghastly—" Hearing the click as the door opened behind her, she stopped. When she turned she saw Campion's tall figure silhouetted against the light from the parlor.

Roderic had gone into the garden to summon them back to the house. Now, seeing Celeste standing in the moonlight—how fetching she was, how incomparably beautiful—unexpectedly he felt as though a hand had reached inside his body, grasped and twisted his heart. His pain was real, not imaginary, a sensation he had never experienced before, a mingling of desire and wonderment and revelation. He started to speak but his throat tightened and words failed him.

Ridiculous! What folly!

He cleared his throat. "Miss Gordon," he said, his voice stiff and punctilious as well as husky, "your aunt is asking for you."

How peculiar. He had meant to invite both of them to return to the parlor but he had spoken only to Rowena. Stepping to one side, he allowed Rowena to enter the house but as Celeste started to walk past him with her head averted, he said, "Wait." When she hesitated, he said, almost desperately, "Please wait."

When still she hesitated, he resisted the urge to reach out and grasp her wrist. Finally she nodded curtly, offering no objection as he closed the door and, when he gestured toward the garden, she followed him back to the sundial now silvered by a waning three-quarter moon that cast its pale light on the surrounding houses, the brick wall and the shrubbery.

Though she could see his face clearly, Celeste found his expression unreadable. Strangely, she had an urge to comfort him but, unsure of herself and unable to find the proper words, she said nothing.

Turning from her, he looked down at the sun dial as his fingers glided idly across the raised numerals. Without glancing up at her, he said, "When a man and a woman are very different one from another, in their backgrounds, their positions in society, their tastes, their habits and their dispositions, as are Prince Lothar and Miss Gordon, 'tis folly for either of them to ever think of becoming more than friends."

Perplexed, she wondered what he was attempting to tell her. Was he really speaking of Rowena or did he in truth refer to her? Was he obliquely warning her never to expect anything more than friendship from him?

To Celeste, her quest for love had become, in a sense, the mirror image of Rowena's. But at least Rowena had the comfort of knowing the prince made no secret of the fact he had fixed his interest on her. Lord Campion revealed little or nothing of his innermost feelings.

Lord Campion must mean exactly what he said, no more and no less—how unlike him such candor was!—and would consider her presumptuous if she read more into his words.

When she made no reply, he asked, "Do you agree?"

She started to nod and say, "Yes," but then vehemently shook her head. "I may have agreed once," she said, "but not now, not in the least."

She heard him draw in his breath—in annoyance, she suspected. Clasping his hands behind his back, he paced to and fro on the far side of the sun dial with his gaze fixed on the garden path.

"You seem to delight in being exasperating," he told her, "in being not only contrary but perverse as well." Suddenly he came to her, stopping in front of her and looking directly at her, the moonglow bathing him in its silver sheen. "Tonight, for instance," he said, "I was taken completely by surprise when Lothar opened Mrs. Atkinson's front door and began calling my name in a voice loud enough to be heard in every nook and cranny of Somers Town."

Recognizing the challenge in his voice, Celeste raised her chin defiantly. "You were surprised because you thought your plot so perfect?"

"I admit I neglected to inquire into the identities of all the various kith and kin of the formidable Mrs. Atkinson. Therefore, no matter what I might have thought, no, the plan was not quite as perfect as I thought. But what troubled me more than half was to find my involvement in the hoax had become such common knowledge."

She realized he was accusing her of betraying him. Annoyed, she said, "If you mean to ask if I informed Rowena, I plead guilty. I discovered I could not, in all good conscience, be a party to your subterfuge."

"Have you forgotten you agreed of your own volition to become my partner?" Taking his quizzing glass in one hand he tapped it against his open palm to emphasize his words. "Agreed to help me end for good and all Lothar's unsuitable alliance? Is this, then, your notion of faithfulness?"

Although she considered herself to be guiltless, Celeste felt her cheeks flame. "Had I the opportunity to tell you what I intended, I certainly would have done so without the slightest hesitation. Unfortunately, I had no chance, none at all. When I informed Rowena of your message, of your plan to lure the prince here, I expected her to refuse to come to Somers Town. You can imagine how surprised and dismayed I was when she decided to drive to Mrs. Atkinson's house tonight. At that time, like you, I had no knowledge of their kinship."

"You quite overwhelm me with your outpouring of words of explanation and justification, Miss Prescott, words signifying little or nothing." He tossed his quizzing glass into the air, caught it with one hand and slipped the glass back into his pocket. "I must assume that you and I are no longer partners. Am I correct?"

"When the time came for me to deceive Rowena, I realized it was impossible to help you with your intrigue. When I originally agreed to your—" She paused, searching for the word that would best show her distaste—"to your rather shabby scheme, I found the idea repugnant, but at the time, I supposed I must suppress my natural inclination to be completely honest in all things."

"Shabby? You call my plan shabby?" Anger harshened his voice. "You never labeled it such when we discussed my ploy at Mrs. Gordon's musical evening. Pray tell me, what led you to change your mind. Was it something I did? Or, perhaps, something I failed to do?"

She frowned, wondering what he meant. "Neither; rather, my feeling about Rowena and the prince changed. She must be allowed to follow her heart without our interference though, as we both realize, she most likely will find unhappiness at the end of her journey."

"What a hopelessly romantic notion," he said scornfully. "Follow her heart indeed! Do all women dwell in fools' paradises? I expect they have little to occupy their minds other than notions of romance, courtship and marriage. Men, on the other hand, Prince Lothar in particular, have more vital concerns to occupy them, affairs of business and of state requiring a sense of diligence, duty and honor. I suppose you believe everyone, yourself included, should follow his heart, that you should toss common sense overboard like so much flotsam as you steer your ship directly onto the reefs of an impossible love."

She drew a deep breath to stem the rising tide of her fury. "Jetsam," she hissed.

"What?"

"Goods thrown overboard are not flotsam. The proper word in this case happens to be jetsam."

"My God." She was gratified to hear the exasperation in his voice. "I see that when your argument fails, you attempt to place a feather in your cap by turning into a dictionary. Jetsam be damned."

"My dear Lord Campion," she said, her voice quivering with fury, "I do not appreciate your sarcasm, nor your insults, nor your oaths. For your information, and despite what you seem to believe, I am not a goose. Should I ever decide on a perilous course such as Rowena follows for myself I would hope to remain sensible enough not to become shipwrecked. As for Rowena, she must be allowed to attempt to avoid those reefs and thus learn from experience. Is that notion so difficult for you to fathom?"

"You, Miss Prescott, are a thin-skinned, prickly, stubborn, wrong-headed woman. I admit I expected much from you; I acknowledge I received but little. Nay, I received nothing. Henceforth, I intend to proceed entirely on my own."

"What you do is no longer my concern; we must follow our separate paths. Let me warn you: deviousness such as yours only serves to create a frightful coil that enmeshes the perpetrator as well as his victims." She folded her arms, staring coldly at him. "I have a great mind to wish you ill, my lord, whatever your new endeavors may be."

"*That* you will soon discover. Only this morning I received a long-awaited letter from Paris; already my coach is on its way to Dover. On its return to town I expect to be able to bring Lothar to his senses."

How smug he was, how self-assured despite tonight's failure. "I urge you to reconsider," she said, alarmed and shaken by his confidence. "Why must you rush hither and thither attempting to thwart two lovers through your nefarious schemes?"

"What I propose to do," he told her, folding his arms across *his* chest, "is best for all concerned. Two months ago I was on my way to visit friends in

Marien-Holstein. I was a contented man, intending to return to England in a fortnight to visit my mother at Courtney Hall in Windermere. King Harlan persuaded me to help him and I consented; I pledged my support. Only an obstinate female such as yourself could fail to understand the rightness of my actions since that time. Be that as it may, I have no desire to remain here to be pelted with your barbs, however elegantly they may be phrased."

So he had examined his motives and his actions and found them good. How high in the instep he was, how god-like he considered himself!

"As I recall," she said icily, "you invited me to remain in the garden, otherwise I would be elsewhere and glad of it. And I shall certainly not stay one moment more!"

She whirled away from him and started toward the door but he strode after her, caught her by the wrist and swung her around to face him. Reaching out with both hands, he gripped her upper arms. She stared up at him, recognized rage in his face and more, a thinly veiled passion that both thrilled and frightened her.

Scarcely able to breathe, she heard the throbbing of her heart as her anger fought against an insidious snake of desire, a terrible longing, an undefined wanting. His hold on her arms eased and she waited, fearful yet expectant, reason warning her to flee from him at the same time her heart bade her stay.

His hand reached to her, lingering on the side of her face in a gentle caress. His fingertips traced a slow path to her mouth, all the while seeming to urge her to come to him, entice her closer and closer. Mesmerized by his touch, she took a step toward him, then another and another until they almost touched, almost and yet not quite.

Suddenly his hand drew back and closed into a fist. He shook his head. "Damn you!" he cried.

Startled, she gasped and shrank away from him as though he had struck her. But her gaze never left his face; she trembled at the sight of his clenched jaw and of his eyes glittering fiercely in the moonlight. Yet it wasn't violence she feared from him but something far more dangerous.

"Damn you," he said once more, his voice much softer than before, his tone almost resigned, as though he had fought a battle with himself and lost. He came to her and, as he enfolded her in his arms, she raised her head to look up at him and as she did his mouth covered hers, his kiss a tantalizing promise.

She closed her eyes, lost and helpless in the sensual glow of his embrace. The night was cool but now, to Celeste, it seemed warm; the garden had yet to emerge from its winter slumber but now, to her, it seemed filled with all the sweetness and radiance of summer.

When his lips left hers she felt the caress of his breath on her lips as he murmured her name over and over, "Celeste, Celeste, Celeste." Instinctively, her hands sought the nape of his neck and she ran her fingers over the softness of his dark hair as she drew his lips down to hers once more. She heard his sharp intake of breath, felt his arms tighten around her, felt the tingling shock as her yearning body molded itself to his.

Once more he kissed her, his lips no longer tender nor caressing but needful, his kiss demanding her response, demanding even more. She returned his kiss, surrendering herself to him as she felt a strange yet wonderful warmth rise and spread within her. She willed the kiss never to end.

Here, she told herself, was where she belonged, enclosed in the circle of his arms for now and forever. Before this moment, without realizing it, she had been incomplete, a lonely wanderer lost in an alien, arid land, but now she had found her oasis, the one place in all the world where she truly belonged.

The tip of his tongue lightly touched her lips, startling her while at the same time sending new quivers of excitement coursing through her body. Emboldened, his tongue traced the contours of her lips. She started to speak his name only to have his tongue invade her mouth and touch her tongue in a caress so daring and so intimate she was thrilled yet alarmed. For an instant she responded before drawing back, afraid.

He suddenly released her and turned to stand with his back to her, his hands clenched at his sides. She could hear his rapid breathing in the stillness of the night. All in a quake, she shivered, her pulses racing, her heart beating wildly.

"Roderic," she whispered, fearful yet wanting him to come to her, to hold and kiss her. To speak her name again, to murmur endearments.

She thought she saw him shake his head. Impulsively, she stepped toward him only to stop at once. What a fool he must think you, she told herself, a schoolgirl swept off her feet by a caress, by a kiss on a garden path.

What had happened to her tonight, Celeste

wondered. Suddenly her world had changed, as a bud changes when it blooms under the warm rays of the summer sun. When he kissed her, she felt free, unfettered, believing all things were possible. At that moment, she realized with dismay, she would have denied him nothing.

The night breeze chilled her and, trembling, she drew her shawl close about her shoulders. How confused her world had become! How upside down everything seemed. In her romantic daydreams she had always pictured a gentleman on his knees, his hands clasping hers as he spoke endearing words of praise, affection and love. Roderic—she no longer thought of him as Lord Campion—had berated her, accused her of betrayal, hurled oaths at her and, after kissing her, said nothing more than her name. Had his easy glibness deserted him?

Bewildered, she stared at him. What must he think of her submitting so docilely to him after the way he had treated her? To not only let him kiss her but to return his kiss with an unseemly passion? If only, by some legerdemain, she could read his thoughts . . .

Roderic was shaken. For his own well-being, for his peace of mind, he had tried to alienate Celeste, had consciously set out to keep her at a safe distance. Hadn't he accused her of betraying him? Of failing him when he needed her most? Of going back on her solemnly pledged word to assist him? He had condemned her not so much to shame her but to protect himself. And he had failed abysmally. At the crucial moment he had been unable to turn his back on her and leave her in her misery.

How weak he was! This woman was unsuitable,

completely so, there could be no question about that. The two of them had little or nothing in common, they hardly spoke the same language. And yet he found his thoughts returning to her night after night, above all else he found himself wanting to see her, to talk to her and, above all, to hold her in his arms and kiss her.

In some mysterious way she made him feel young again, like a green lad of nineteen or twenty with all the world yet to conquer, she forced him to question and almost be shamed by his cynicism, made him believe it possible that the world could be a better place, that men with vision and ideals might triumph after all. And, more importantly, that he could be one of those men.

What was going through her mind at this moment? She had obstinately defended her betrayal, had given voice to a great many romantic and absolutely impractical notions. What did she think of him? And how strange that he found himself seeking her approval. In all likelihood she considered him an obstacle to be surmounted for the sake of her friend, Rowena, someone to be cajoled and eventually persuaded through the clever use of her feminine wiles. As he nearly had been.

His course, though, was set. Hadn't he given his word to King Harlan? He meant to carry out his part of that bargain, come what may. As for Celeste—he no longer thought of her as Miss Prescott—he would let fate decide. What would be, would be.

He looked down at her—how lovely she looked in the soft moonglow!—and the sight of her caused him to catch his breath, made him forget every one of his good intentions. He took a step toward her, she advanced a step toward him, and then the door to the house opened and Lothar and Rowena walked into the garden.

Roderic turned to them. How fortunate their arrival. They had saved him from himself. Why, then, did he wish they had never appeared?

Chapter 15

"I have a fit of the dismals," Rowena said, kneading her forehead with her fingertips. "Perhaps a visit to Glaffney's will provide the cure."

"Glaffney's?" Celeste asked. "Is that an apothecary's?"

Rowena smiled wanly. "No, Mr. Glaffney is the milliner on Tottenham Court Road where mama and I have shopped for years and years. Spring surprised me this year; I find myself without a hat to wear."

It was early afternoon and they were in the Gordon drawing room. During the several days that had passed since their visit to Somers Town, Rowena's moods had swung like a pendulum from elation to the deepest gloom.

"Ostrich feathers are quite the thing this year," Rowena went on. "I fancy a quite extravagant bonnet with three or four lovely plumes. Nothing is more cheering than a new hat for spring. Unless it be two new hats."

Celeste could imagine Roderic raising an eyebrow and saying, "My observation is that shopping is the cure-all for every *malaise* known to womankind."

And she could hear herself answering, "On the other hand, with gentlemen the cure-all for melancholy would seem to be several overdoses of strong drink. Which of the two remedies do you judge to be the least harmful, my lord?"

Desist, she instructed herself, *you must stop these imaginary conversations with Roderic—they have become much too frequent and serve no purpose except to depress your own spirits.*

"Shall we drive to Glaffney's without delay?" Rowena asked and, when Celeste nodded her approval, she rang for Harkins.

Minutes later they were rattling over the stones of Oxford Street. Rowena nattered on in an almost feverish way, not only speculating on the elegant bonnets adorned with plumes and artificial flowers they would find at Glaffney's but also describing the latest Paris fashions in gowns, gloves and sandal shoes she had seen pictured in *La Belle Assemblée.* "My own gown," she said, lifting a fold of material between her gloved thumb and forefinger, "is outrageously dowdy."

Celeste, who had been listening with but half an ear, glanced in surprise at her companion's long-sleeved white muslin sprigged in lavender and green with lavender satin flounces at the hem and a matching ruffle along the scoop neck. To Celeste, the gown seemed modest yet fetching, and most becoming.

As for herself, Celeste was more than content with

her loden green gown featuring the new short puffed sleeves. To her mind the three narrow bands of forest green satin braid and a fringe of the same color at the hem added a touch of elegance, especially since the green satin band was repeated at the modified vee neck. Because of the short sleeves she carried a cashmere shawl in a pale green that matched her parasol.

Suddenly Rowena stopped talking in mid-sentence. Celeste glanced at her friend and, when she found her staring straight in front of her with a stricken look on her face, she followed her gaze, placing a comforting hand on Rowena's arm even though she saw nothing out of the ordinary on the street ahead of them.

"Whatever is the matter?" Celeste asked.

Rowena sighed. "I do try to occupy my mind with pleasant thoughts but how can I? Lothar wrote to tell me his uncle arrives in London either today or tomorrow. In fact, he may be in town at this very moment. How can I help but be all aflutter? Lothar swears that neither the King's entreaties nor his threats will alter his feeling for me but, alas, his actions may well contradict his feelings. What a maddening mull this is."

"Lothar has never disappointed you before, not once. If you recall, he adamantly refused to be persuaded by Roderic's arguments."

"Roderic?" Rowena looked sharply at Celeste, raising her eyebrows at the familiar use of his name. "As a matter of fact, Lord Campion did succeed in swaying him with his talk of a prince's duty to his country and to his people but, yes, Lothar finally managed to stand firm against his lordship's mischief-making."

"And he will again," Celeste said with more confidence than she felt. "Nothing will deter him." Not even Roderic, she assured herself.

She had heard nothing from Roderic since their stolen moments in the garden at Somers Town. Although he had told her he intended to go forward with his plans to separate the prince and Rowena, surely what had passed between them in the garden must have softened his heart. To please her, wouldn't he be apt to abandon his efforts to thwart the lovers? In his place, she would not persist; surely he must have had second thoughts after hearing her objections.

"If I had followed her advice," Rowena was saying, "my life would have been so simple."

"Forgive me," Celeste said, "I fear I was woolgathering. Whose advice? And what would have made your life simple?"

"Marrying Mr. Hugh B. Garson, of course. Mama strongly advised me to accept his proposal and I had no strong objections to Hubie. Nor do I now. Perhaps he loved me enough to make up for my not loving him at all."

Celeste wondered if such an imbalance of affection ever made for a contented marriage. "Do you actually wish you had married him?" she asked.

"No, certainly not. Yet all my might-have-beens and if-onlys have a disconcerting way of crossing my mind when I suffer a fit of the dismals."

Their carriage slowed to a stop and after a moment Harkins opened the door and said, "Begging your pardon, Miss Gordon, but there's a barricade of sorts across the street. 'Pears like some construction work."

"Glaffney's is only a short walk from here," Rowena said, stepping down from the carriage and opening her parasol, "merely around the corner."

They were soon halted by a rope across the walkway. "Glaffney's?" a man superintending the work on the roadway repeated in reply to Rowena's question. "That shop's long since shuttered," he said. When Rowena stared in surprise, he added, "To make way for the Regent's new thoroughfare to the park, you see."

For a moment, Celeste thought her friend was about to break into tears but Rowena drew in a deep breath, letting it out with a sigh. "Nothing lasts these days, nothing endures," she lamented as they walked back to the carriage, "not even Glaffney's. It must be that Mr. John Nash. They say he found a London built of good solid brick but won't be satisfied until he leaves nothing behind him but a stucco that flakes and peels and cracks. Mr. Nash builds for today, not tomorrow."

"Perhaps," Celeste said, "because he agrees with Mr. Sydney Smith. 'Why should I care about doing something for posterity?' Mr. Smith wished to know. 'What has posterity ever done for me?'"

Rowena stared at her. "How cynical," she said. "Do you know who you reminded me of just then? The voice is yours, Celeste, but the words are the words of Lord Campion."

A vivid flush spread across Celeste's face. She started to deny the truth of what Rowena said but hesitated as she wondered if it could be true. To her great relief, Rowena failed to notice her confusion since at that moment her attention was drawn to a curricle driving pell-mell in their direction with a gentleman wearing a dazzling red and orange uniform at the reins.

"Lothar!" Rowena cried as the prince swung down from his carriage and came to bow over their hands, retaining Rowena's well past the dictates of politeness.

When Celeste started to leave them to walk ahead to the Gordon carriage, Lothar said, much to her surprise, "No, please stay, Miss Prescott," and proceeded to launch into a lengthy and, to her, not very interesting explanation of how he had come to find them here. To Celeste, he appeared up in the boughs with excitement and yet at the same time strangely ill-at-ease.

"Such a dashing figure you make in your uniform," Celeste said, admiring the prince's plumed hat, sword and mirror-like black boots. "This is the first time I've seen you wear it."

Her innocent remark seemed to unsettle the prince even more. After an uneasy glance at Rowena, he said to Celeste, "I have the honor to be the captain of the Marien-Holstein Palace Guard."

"The sum and substance of the matter is that your uncle has arrived in London," Rowena said matter-of-factly.

"He has indeed. My uncle, the king, arrived yesterday and later this afternoon he and I are invited to a reception at Carlton House where King Harlan expects to have a last opportunity to urge the British to sign the naval treaty. Alas, since Lord Howell has not yet returned to town, our mission appears futile."

Lothar proceeded to expound at tedious length on the King's retinue, the King's hope that an heir to his throne would arrive early in the autumn and the King's impressions of London after his long absence from the city. Rowena nodded rather impatiently now and again but had little to say, leaving the burden of their side of the conversation to Celeste.

At last Lothar fell silent. He looked down at his gleaming black boots, he shifted his weight from one foot to the other, in fact he seemed to be summoning his courage to bid them an abrupt good-bye. But if so, why on earth had he hurried here to see them, Celeste wondered—only to change his mind and remark on the mildness of the weather for this time of year.

"And what of your Mr. Wyche?" Rowena asked somewhat abruptly. "I believe you meant to visit him yesterday."

"Ah, yes, Wyche. I drove to John Street yesterday afternoon only to discover that Mr. Samuel Wyche has changed residences. Rather suddenly and, perhaps, surreptitiously as well, since none of his former neighbors seemed to have any notion as to when he went or where."

"Do you mean," Rowena asked in dismay, "that Mr. Wyche has disappeared? And your money has vanished as well? Not to put too fine a point on it, that gentleman seems to be monstrously wicked."

"All this is a misunderstanding, no more." Lothar, Celeste noted, spoke without his usual conviction. "I expect him to appear at any moment. The last time I spoke to Mr. Wyche he exuded confidence. Besides,

Roderic believes he might be able to locate him."

"Roderic!" Rowena sniffed. "His lordship is more harm than help, it appears to me. Besides being a master of deception, his only talent seems to be a curious ability to peddle your country's Roemermann Soap to shops all across England."

Lothar shrugged and raised his hands either in despair or apology for his friend or, perhaps, Celeste thought, in sheer desperation. He certainly gave the impression of a man beset from all sides.

Finally, with his gaze fixed somewhere above and beyond them, he blurted, "I must return to Marien-Holstein on Friday next. Only for a short while, until the crisis passes. If we have no naval treaty, my country is thrown into great danger, so the king plans to mobilize the army and the navy. Duty demands I report to my post, with the Palace Guard."

Rowena paled. "If you leave England now," she told him, "you'll never return. Never." She seemed more resigned than angry, as though she had secretly given up hope long ago.

"Not true," Lothar insisted. "You have my word, I give you my solemn oath in the presence of Miss Prescott. You must have faith in my steadfastness, Rowena."

Celeste, hearing the uncertainty in his voice, wished herself miles away. The last thing in the world she wanted was to be a witness to this unhappy confrontation.

Shaking her head sadly, Rowena turned away from him. "That's all well and good," she said, "but I expect I've always known it would end like this. Even though once, nay, more than once, I dared hope—" She broke off, suppressing a sob.

Lothar started to reach out to her but stopped, biting his lip. He awkwardly brought forth his pocket watch, looking down at it in seeming amazement. "My God," he said, "where has the time flown? I have no choice but to leave you now. The reception at Carlton House. The king. The naval treaty."

He bowed over Celeste's hand and then touched Rowena on the arm but again she shook her head, refusing to either speak to him or look at him. His helpless expression as he glanced at Celeste might have gained her sympathy were it not for her loyalty to Rowena. His position was unenviable, a man trapped between his allegiance to his country and his loyalty to a woman he loved. She could offer him no help so when she shook her head he at last turned away and hurried to his curricle.

After driving his carriage around to return the way he had come, Lothar raised his hat and called to them. *"Auf wiedersehen,"* he said as he flicked the reins. Celeste started: it was the first time she had heard him speak in his native tongue. In a way, she realized, he had already returned to Marien-Holstein.

Though she'd refused to look at him a few minutes before, Rowena watched his curricle until it was out of sight, then, shoulders slumping, slowly folded her parasol and returned to the carriage.

As soon as they were on their way back to the Gordon town house, Celeste said softly, "Don't despair. The British may decide to sign the naval treaty after all so the prince will be able to remain in

London and win over his uncle and all will be well for both of you. Greater miracles have happened."

Rowena said nothing and when Celeste glanced at her friend she saw tears brimming in her eyes; even Celeste herself realized her words of encouragement represented little more than wishful thinking. She so wanted Rowena to be happy! When she took her companion's hand, Rowena rested her head on Celeste's shoulder and they drove the rest of the way home in a cheerless silence.

At dinner that evening Rowena shifted her food about her plate but ate little while saying almost nothing. On the rare occasions she spoke it was mainly to recall Glaffney's glory in days gone by when she and her mother had so enjoyed shopping there. She lauded the courtesy of the clerks, the stylishness of the bonnets and the more than reasonable prices. And now, she lamented, Glaffney's was no more. There might be other fine milliners' shops in London but there would never be another Glaffney's.

"Never," Rowena repeated sadly. "What's past is past."

Rowena might speak of the demise of Glaffney's, Celeste realized, but her thoughts must be on the imminent departure of the prince and her justifiable worry he'd never return.

Promising to join Celeste later that evening in the drawing room, Rowena retired to her bed chamber immediately after dinner. Celeste tried to read a novel while sitting in front of the fire—the nights were still damp and chilling despite the warmer weather—but, concerned about her friend, her mind wandered until she finally laid the book aside and stared disconsolately at the fitful flames.

She was about to seek out Rowena when Harkins entered the room. "Lord Campion," he announced. Celeste's heart leaped with anticipation.

Roderic strode through the doorway and across the room, bowing and raising her hand to his lips. He positioned a straight-backed chair in front of her, sat down facing her and leaned forward with his elbows on his knees, his gaze meeting hers. "Since I intend to be completely honest with you, to behave honorably at all times and in all things," he said, "I hastened here to tell you myself, so you wouldn't hear the news tomorrow from others."

Pleasurably unsettled by his unexpected visit, at first his words blurred in her mind until she forced herself to concentrate on what he was saying. She would be the first to know, he had told her; he wanted to be honest with her. She waited expectantly for him to go on.

"I attended this afternoon's reception at Carlton House," he said. "King Harlan raised the question of the naval treaty but he was, I fear, rebuffed. In very diplomatic language, of course, with no offense intended or, I suppose, given, but yet he left just as empty-handed as he arrived."

"I expected the worst, as did Rowena," Celeste admitted. She waited, wondering if this unremarkable news was what he had come to tell her. Surely not.

"You may recall," he said, "that when last we met I mentioned receiving a letter from Paris."

She nodded, remembering that the letter had to do

with one of his schemes to counter the prince's partiality for Rowena. Had he come to her tonight to tell her he'd finally abandoned his efforts? It thrilled her to believe he had changed his mind to please her. Very likely that was the case or he might even be intending to promise, for her sake, to do everything in his power to convince the prince's uncle of Rowena's suitability.

"The letter," he went on, "was from the young woman I've attempted to communicate with ever since I returned to London from Marien-Holstein. My original letters to Stuttgart, it turns out, had been redirected to Paris, where they only recently reached the object of my search."

Stuttgart? Why had Roderic been writing to a young woman in Germany? Celeste frowned in consternation as a possible reason occurred to her. "And who is this mysterious young woman?" she demanded.

He reached to her but, knowing all would be lost if she ever allowed him to touch her, she sprang to her feet and retreated to the far side of the sofa where she stood with both hands resting on its back. Roderic rose slowly to his feet and, his gaze meeting hers, drew in a deep breath.

"The young woman is the Princess Hildegarde," he told her.

Lothar's betrothed! She had feared as much. So, despite her objections, Roderic had gone ahead with his plans. Did she, then, mean so little to him? Angry and disappointed, Celeste stared at him in dismay as a feeling of loss and emptiness engulfed her.

"Princess Hildegarde had journeyed to Paris,"

Roderic said hurriedly as though anxious to have done with the matter as quickly as possible, "where my urgent messages finally reached her. I suggested she come to London at my expense and she accepted my invitation by return post. The Princess Hildegarde arrives tonight; I meet her on the morrow to bring her to Lothar."

"How diligent you are in your matchmaking! If you were equipped with wings I might very well mistake you for an English cupid."

Roderic frowned. "As you are aware," he said, "the prince has been ordered to return to Marien-Holstein. And he will return, since his first allegiance has always been to his country, have no doubt of that. What could be more agreeable than for him to have, at the same time, the comfort and support of a suitable wife?"

How could he possibly be so blind to Lothar's feelings for Rowena? As for poor Rowena, Roderic behaved as though she didn't even exist.

"In your view, the prince's wishes count for less than naught," she said tartly. "Any female will do as long as you judge her suitable and believe her able to provide comfort and support. You sound like a carriage maker preparing to install cushions."

He scowled. "And you, my dear Celeste, sound like a shrew. Remember, if you will, that all through this affair the constant one has been myself. You vacillated back and forth, changing your mind time and time again, first siding with me and then turning against me, whilst I remained firm in my goals and the means to achieve them."

"Constant, yes, but what honor is there in being

constant in the pursuit of misguided goals? None at all."

He reached out his hand. "Come here," he said.

She shook her head, watching him warily while her pulses raced. How could she be so terribly disappointed and so furious while at the same time she ached for his touch?

Roderic slowly advanced on the sofa that separated them, his hand still extended toward her. She stood firm even though she realized he meant to unfairly counter her arguments with kisses. She longed for him to take her in his arms and to hold her but, no, she wouldn't fall into that trap again.

He knelt on the sofa cushion and reached toward her but at the last moment she stepped back. He lunged for her, the sofa tipped over with a crash and he tumbled forward onto the carpet.

She gasped, her hand flying to her mouth, afraid he might be hurt even as she backed toward the door. Roderic pushed himself to his feet. Assured he was all right, she suddenly felt a most inappropriate amusement which she feared might lead to unforgivable laughter. Turning, she fled across the hall to the stairs, looking over her shoulder to see Roderic come to the doorway of the drawing room where he stood glaring at her but making no effort to pursue her.

As she started up the stairs, she thought she glimpsed the flick of a green skirt above her and all thought of laughter fled. Rowena had worn green. Could Rowena have come downstairs and overheard what Roderic had told her? She fervently hoped not.

When she reached the top of the stairs, however, she saw no one in the upper hall. Hastening to her friend's bed chamber, she tapped insistently on the door. "Rowena?" she called.

After a pause, Rowena said, "Celeste? I took a draught for my headache and so I intend to retire early. Good-night."

Still uneasy, Celeste had no choice but to answer, "Sleep well."

She made her way to her own room with a heavy heart. Roderic had not only betrayed his good friend, the prince, he had betrayed her. How little he must care for her to ignore her protests and proceed blithely with his schemes. How she wished there was a way for her to take him down a peg. Or two or three.

In the morning, Rowena failed to appear for breakfast. Perturbed, Celeste was about to go in search of her when Alice, Rowena's maid, hurried into the room, a frightened look on her face. "Miss Gordon's bed weren't slept in," she said. "I found this on her pillow, and made out your name on it." She handed Celeste a sealed letter.

Tearing open the letter, Celeste scanned the scrawled message with growing alarm:

> *Dear Celeste, it has become all too hopeless. I cannot bear any more. I must leave. Tell mama I am safe and not to worry.*
>
> *All my love, Rowena.*

Chapter 16

As she finished reading Rowena's letter, Celeste tried to tamp down a rush of panic, realizing that only by remaining calm in the face of this catastrophe could she help her friend. Damn Roderic and his schemes!

Now there was no doubt in her mind that Rowena had overheard him the evening before as he trumpeted the news of his letter from Paris. The arrival of the prince's betrothed in London in conjunction with Lothar's imminent departure for Marien-Holstein had been too much for Rowena to bear. And so she had fled. Certainly Rowena had behaved foolishly, yet Celeste wondered if there was anyone, herself included, who might not have done the same when faced with a similar predicament.

Rowena had fled, but where had she gone? Celeste was confident her friend had no intention of harming herself. No, Rowena had told the simple truth, at least as she saw it, when she wrote she was safe. Where was she then? Had she sought sanctuary with her aunt in Somers Town? Celeste shook her head. An unlikely choice; Celeste, could not imagine seeking asylum with the rather frivolous and saucy Mrs. Jeanne Atkinson.

Celeste closed her eyes as she tried to recall the details of their conversation the day before on their drive to Glaffney's, hoping something Rowena had said would provide a clue to her whereabouts. Suddenly Celeste gasped.

How simple life would be if I were married to Mr. Hugh B. Garson.

Those might not have been Rowena's exact words but that was certainly the sum and substance of what she had said. Could Rowena have gone to Hubie Garson? That gentleman might maintain an overflowing kennel but he was partial to Rowena and had appeared to Celeste to be amiable, attractive and wealthy. This pleasing combination of attributes might prove irresistible to an overwrought Rowena.

Summoning Harkins, Celeste told him in confidence exactly what had happened. When he could shed no light on Rowena's possible whereabouts, she said, "I intend to write to inform Mrs. Gordon at once."

In her letter to Rowena's mother, she concealed nothing that had occurred while at the same time doing her best to be reassuring. As soon as she saw Harkins on his way to post her letter to Brighton, she penned a brief note to Prince Lothar.

By the time she handed a neighborhood lad five pence to deliver her message to the prince, Harkins had returned. Should she leave at once in search of Rowena or should she wait for the prince to come to her assistance? Although certain he would hasten to her as soon as her message reached him, she had no way of knowing when that might be. She decided to wait an hour but not one minute more.

The prince, accompanied by Roderic, arrived at the Gordon town house forty minutes later in a coach and four. The prince appeared flustered and overwrought while Roderic, though calm and collected, eyed her warily, as if uncertain whether her vexation of the evening before had subsided. For her part, Celeste was determined to be icily polite to him, no less but certainly no more.

"Why in the name of heaven would she run off?" the prince demanded.

This was no time to attempt to soften the blow, Celeste decided. "Rowena despaired," she told him, "when you seemed determined to return to Marien-Holstein without her." She made no mention of Roderic's summoning the Princess Hildegarde from Paris since she had no proof positive Rowena had overheard him.

The prince reddened. As well he should, Celeste told herself. The crisis precipitated by the king's arrival had shown him to be less than stalwart.

"This flight gives every evidence," Roderic put in, "of being little more than a female ruse. Miss Gordon is seeking to elicit your sympathy by feigning a greater distress than she feels."

"Not true," Celeste snapped back at him. "How unfair you are. What could *you,* or the prince either, possibly know of the anguish a woman feels when the man she loves seems about to abandon her?"

The prince evidently agreed with her for he glared at Roderic before turning to Celeste. "Have you any notion where she might have gone?" he asked.

"I have been thinking of little else," she told him. "Yesterday, on our drive to Glaffney's, Rowena did make mention of a Mr. Hugh B. Garson."

"Hubie Garson?" Roderic asked. "That tiresome fellow with the hundred wolfhounds?"

The prince's face darkened but then he shook his head and wrinkled his nose as, Celeste was certain, he imagined being in the presence of one hundred dogs. "Rowena would never go to him. Never in a thousand years."

"You and Roderic may not appreciate dogs," Celeste said, "but many people do. I happen to be one of them."

"I have nothing against dogs," Roderic said, "just as I have nothing against children; in fact, I enjoy children, I find them charming. But that doesn't mean I desire one hundred of them."

"I suspect the tales of Mr. Garson's hundred dogs are greatly exaggerated," Celeste said.

Roderic shrugged. "Whether they are or not, we must always keep this maxim in mind: There is absolutely no foretelling what a woman might or might not do when she discovers herself in a muddle."

"Where might we find this Garson?" the prince asked.

"Harkins supplied me with directions," Celeste

told him, deciding to ignore Roderic's easy dismissal of Rowena's heartbreak. "He resides at 45 Brook Street."

Roderic swung his cane in a horizontal arc as though it was a dowsing rod seeking the location not of water but of Mr. Hugh B. Garson. When the cane finally came to point in a northeasterly direction, he held it steady and said, "Brook Street is but a short distance from here. Miss Gordon could have left this house and walked to Hubie Garson's in a matter of minutes."

"No!" Lothar was adamant. "In the middle of the night? To seek succor at a gentleman's house? Never, I tell you. Not Rowena. Pray remember, I know her better than either of you do."

"Not well enough, however," Roderic pointed out, "to envision her running off into the night without a word of warning. So you may be equally mistaken as to her destination. At the very least, Lothar, we should visit Hubie and thus settle the matter for good and all."

Lothar frowned, he shook his head, he looked to Celeste for support but, finding none, he said with a sigh, "To Garson's, then."

Celeste wondered if his reluctance arose not from a firm belief they would fail to find Rowena with Mr. Garson but rather from a fear they might. She said nothing more, however, until it became evident the two gentlemen were planning to drive to Brook Street without her.

"I intend to accompany you," she insisted. "Rowena was my responsibility, her mother placed her in my care and I intend to help search for her until we find her and bring her safely home."

Roderic frowned, Lothar shrugged; neither, though, raised an objection when she walked between them to the coach. They soon arrived at the Garson residence at 45 Brook Street, a magnificent white marble mansion in Greek revival style with four columns across the front rising three stories high. Smoke curled from several of the many chimneys symmetrically placed on the roofs while a semicircular portico graced the right side of the building.

"A splendid example of English architecture," Roderic said on their way up the marble steps to the front door.

"Pretentious," Lothar murmured when they were greeted by the butler.

As they were escorted down a long hallway, two Irish setters joined them and trotted at Celeste's side, pausing to listen when they were announced and entering the drawing room with them. Mr. Hugh B. Garson placed his pipe on a table, rose from his chair and advanced to welcome them. Though not handsome, Celeste thought he had an intriguing face, rounded and rather pugnacious. In later years he might well come to resemble an English bulldog.

Lothar explained the reason for their unanticipated visit.

"Rowena missing?" Celeste was certain that Mr. Garson could never have feigned his look of shocked surprise. "You thought I might have a notion as to her whereabouts? If only I did!"

"I knew we would never find Rowena here," the prince muttered.

"Yet we must consider every possibility." Roderic turned to Mr. Garson. "Pray think man, think. Where might she have gone?"

While Celeste was watching Mr. Garson, his hands clasped behind his back and his head lowered, pace back and forth in front of the hearth, one of the setters came to her and nuzzled her hand. Dropping to her knees, she stroked and hugged the handsome dog.

"I say!" She looked up to find Mr. Garson smiling down at her. "You like dogs, then?" he asked.

"Oh, yes. My father died when I was very young but I can still remember him holding me in his arms while showing me his foxhounds. Ever since I was a child I've wanted a dog of my own, but I've never had a place to keep one."

"The setter who has taken such an obvious liking to you is Jupiter," he said, "while the other one is Apollo. I name all my dogs for gods and goddesses."

"You have a pantheon of canines," Roderic remarked.

Celeste resisted an impulse to look at Roderic to see the scornful expression she knew must be on his face.

Mr. Garson did dart a glance at Roderic. "I never make an exception," he told him. "With that in mind, I intend to name the pick of my next litter Celeste."

Touché! Celeste thought even as she blushed.

"May I?" Mr. Garson asked, reaching down, taking Celeste's hand and helping her to her feet. After holding her hand an instant longer than necessary, he stepped back. "I say!" As though seeing her for the first time, he looked admiringly at her simple white muslin gown from its lace hem to its scalloped neckline. "That *is* a fetching frock!"

Before she could acknowledge the compliment, Roderic interrupted, his voice fretful. "Mr. Garson," he said, "appears to have forgotten the reason for our presence here. Would I be very much remiss to remind him of Miss Gordon's disappearance?"

"Mr. Garson is well aware of the need for haste," Mr. Garson said. "Some of us, myself included, have the ability to consider several matters at one and the same time. After searching my memory, I can only suggest that Rowena must have gone to stay with one of her aunts."

"I know of two aunts, Jessamine and Jeanne," Roderic said. "Are there perchance more?"

"At least two more," Lothar put in impatiently. "I recall meeting both Jezebel and June and I've heard Rowena speak of others."

Mr. Garson nodded. "I believe Rowena is blessed with a total of six aunts," he said. "And all with given names beginning with the letter 'J'. The aunt who lives closest to Brook Street makes her home somewhere in Somers Town."

"That would be the widow Atkinson," Celeste said. "Since Lord Campion happens to be a great favorite of hers," she added, glancing at Roderic and finding him frowning, "I expect he could easily charm her into telling us whatever she knows."

"Just so," Lothar said. "We will drive to Mrs. Atkinson's at once. I recall the way only too well."

"And I will follow you in my landau," Mr. Garson said.

"We appreciate your offer of assistance, Mr. Garson," Roderic said in a tone that told Celeste he didn't appreciate it in the least, "but there's no need for you to trouble yourself. The prince and I can manage quite well, thank you just the same."

"Ah, but my dear Lord Campion, you may not have considered the fact that the widow Atkinson may provide us with several possible destinations for Rowena. With but one carriage you would have to visit them consecutively; with two carriages, mine and yours, you will be able to visit them simultaneously and thus save valuable time." He turned to Celeste. "Do you see the logic of my suggestion, Miss Prescott?"

"I most decidedly do, Mr. Garson," she said without hesitation.

"We have no time for haggling," Lothar said to Roderic. "By all means join us if you wish, Mr. Garson."

"Are you familiar with the route to Mrs. Atkinson's?" Mr. Garson asked Celeste.

"I believe I could find my way there."

"Then you must accompany me in my landau to serve as my guide," Mr. Garson said. Turning to Roderic, he added, "In the event my coachman fails to keep pace with yours. Addams has an unfortunate habit of becoming confused in the swirl of London."

Celeste was about to decline the offer but, recalling how Roderic and Lothar had been prepared to set off in search of Rowena without her, changed her mind in the twinkling of an eye. "I accept with thanks," she told Mr. Garson. She glanced at Roderic but found him seemingly engrossed in studying a hunting print on the wall.

As soon as Mr. Garson left them to make the arrangements, however, Roderic swung around and came to her. Breathless, she stared up at him, not knowing what to expect. Something about him always set her pulses racing and there seemed to be nothing on earth that she could do about it. Nor was she certain she wanted to.

"I say!" Roderic's imitation of Mr. Garson was devastatingly accurate. "May I?" he asked Celeste.

Without waiting for her answer, he plucked something from her sleeve and when he held it up between his thumb and forefinger to look at it through his quizzing glass, she recognized the long reddish dog hair. He released the hair and watched, as though fascinated, while it drifted to the carpet.

Celeste searched for a cutting rejoinder but, caught somewhere between amusement and annoyance, found herself speechless. She was rescued by Mr. Garson's return and soon found herself sitting beside him in his elegant carriage as they drove north toward Somers Town.

Her curiosity forced her to ask, "Is it true you own one hundred dogs?"

"No," he said, "not true at all. At the last accounting I had seven at Brook Street and sixty-two at my Highland Manor House in Surrey."

Unable to think of an appropriate comment—after all, even sixty-nine dogs was rather outside of enough—she remained silent.

"I breed dogs, I raise dogs, and I hunt with dogs," he said earnestly. "I realize there are those who deride my love of those noble animals. Some of these naysayers are the very same gentlemen and ladies who fill their homes with oil paintings, bring statuary back to England from Italy to clutter their lawns or boast of their collections of snuffboxes. Have you ever seen a snuffbox that could follow the scent of a fox, or herd a flock of sheep, or guard a home or provide a man with loyal companionship?"

She shook her head. "Certainly not," she said.

"But I have no need to convince you of the merits of man's best friend, Miss Prescott. The two of us have a great deal in common."

When they arrived in Somers Town, Mr. Garson was praising the attributes of his Highland Manor House dogs. By the time they were driving along Duke's Row he was hinting that he would be more than pleased to extend an invitation so Celeste could become personally acquainted with them.

As soon as they were all settled in Mrs. Atkinson's parlor, the widow, answering Lothar's question, said emphatically, "Have I seen Rowena in the last two days? No, not hide nor hair of her."

"Have you any notion at all where she might be?" Lothar asked. Celeste noticed that the prince's distress increased with every passing minute.

Mrs. Atkinson bit her lip as she thought. Suddenly her face brightened and her mouth flew open. Celeste expected her to speak but instead she shook her head, obviously discomfited.

"If you have any ideas at all," Lothar beseeched her, "for God's sake tell us."

"Jennifer Barnes," Mrs. Atkinson said after a moment's hesitation. "Jennifer, now she's my oldest sister. She disgraced us all, Jennifer did, she humiliated the family. The very thought of what she did still makes me want to hang my head in shame."

"What on earth did she do?" Roderic wanted to know.

"She married a yeoman. Well-to-do of late, mind you, but still Jethro's a tiller of the soil for all his money. His farm's near Islington; Rowena loved visiting there when she was a child and so knew no better."

"By all means give us directions," Lothar said.

"With your permission," Mrs. Atkinson told him, "I'll go with you. It's been months since I last saw Jennifer. No matter what she may have done, she's still one of the family and, to my mind, blood's always been thicker than water."

"Excellent." Lothar offered her his arm. "You shall ride in my carriage and show us the way."

As they left the parlor, Mrs. Atkinson turned to Roderic. "Allow me to adjust your cravat, my lord," she said. Going to him, she straightened his neckpiece.

And, Celeste thought angrily as she stalked to Mr. Garson's landau, Roderic appeared to enjoy every lingering moment of the widow's attention. She even suspected he might have deliberately disarranged his cravat. Not that she cared what he did.

After a drive of less than thirty minutes the two

carriages clattered into the Barnes' yard to the clucking of scattering chickens and the barking of mongrel dogs. They stopped in front of the farmhouse—a substantial thatched-roof structure—and when Roderic rapped on the door it was opened by a grey-haired woman. She stared dubiously at them.

"My dear, dear Jennifer," Mrs. Atkinson said, coming forward. "How very nice to see you again after all these many months."

For a moment Jennifer regarded her city sister with an expression that told Celeste she detected insincerity in the effusive greeting. After a slight hesitation, though, she opened her arms and the sisters embraced. Disengaging herself rather hurriedly, Mrs. Atkinson performed a hasty round of introductions.

"We come seeking your niece, Rowena," Lothar said.

Saying nothing in reply, Jennifer Barnes turned and walked away from them, leaving the door ajar. Lothar walked across the sill and they all trooped after Mrs. Barnes along a dark hall to a spacious and sunny kitchen at the rear of the house.

Mrs. Barnes stepped to one side and Celeste, looking past her, gasped with relief as she saw Rowena sitting at a table where she and her aunt had evidently been taking tea. Rowena sprang to her feet, her gaze on Lothar; he started toward her but stopped; they stared silently, longingly, at one another for what seemed an eternity before throwing themselves into each other's arms.

When at last Lothar released her he kept one arm around Rowena's waist as he turned to face the others. "I wish to say this to one and all, so no one will misunderstand my feelings or my intentions. I love Rowena, have loved her for many months. Though I intend to honor my obligation to my country by returning to Marien-Holstein, I shall return there with Rowena Gordon as my bride."

Celeste felt a glow of pleasure for her friend. However innocently, Rowena had forced the prince to realize the depth of his feelings and given him the courage to act with honor. She glanced at Roderic and found him standing with his arms folded, his face without expression.

"I set one condition, however," Lothar went on, giving Celeste a turn. Was he about to waver, she wondered.

"If she will have me," he said. "Will you Rowena? Will you marry me?"

"Oh, yes," she said. "Yes, yes, yes." He kissed her to applause and murmurs of approval.

"And now we shall return to town," Lothar said, "to spread the glorious news."

After several rounds of congratulations and best wishes, after they all said their good byes to Mrs. Barnes, they left the farmhouse.

"Celeste must come with me," Rowena insisted as they walked toward the two carriages.

"Perhaps," Roderic said to Mr. Garson, "you could drive Mrs. Atkinson to Somers Town."

Mr. Garson appeared ready to object but then bowed his consent. "By the bye, Campion," he said with a malicious gleam in his eye, "I do like that new soap of yours."

"It is not *my* soap." Roderic's tone was icy. "It is a Marien-Holstein soap, it is Mr. Roemermann's soap, but it is not *mine.*"

"As you wish," Mr. Garson said, suppressing a smile as he offered his hand to assist Mrs. Atkinson.

"I understand you breed dogs, Mr. Garson," the widow said as she settled herself in the landau. "I love dogs and think most highly of gentlemen who appreciate them. I expect you could teach me a great deal about dogs."

Celeste thought she heard Roderic mutter under his breath, "But very little about breeding."

As soon as they took facing seats in the prince's coach for the drive south into town, Lothar put his arm around Rowena's shoulders and she nestled against him. Though overjoyed at her friend's happiness, Celeste couldn't help comparing it to her own despair made more than evident by the fact that she sat in one corner of their seat while Roderic occupied the other.

After they had traveled several miles, Roderic said, "After days of wrestling with my conscience and taking into consideration all that you, Lothar, and you, Celeste, have said, I have reconsidered. Lothar, I now believe you should marry Rowena whether your uncle approves or not."

Lothar leaned forward and clapped his friend on the shoulder. "Capital!" he cried, beaming with pleasure. Rowena, however, appeared skeptical while Celeste wavered between doubt concerning Roderic's good intentions and elation at his change of heart.

"Now," Lothar said, "I have only to win over King Harlan when I see him tomorrow. And find a way to raise some of the ready if he cuts the purse strings as he threatens to do. Unfortunately, as yet there has been no word whatever from Mr. Samuel Wyche."

"What time do you meet your uncle?" Roderic wanted to know.

"At three in the afternoon. And I intend to bring Rowena with me."

"Then allow me to call on you at two," Roderic said. "I may have a few pleasant surprises for you."

Celeste gave him a frowning look. Any surprises must concern Mr. Wyche and the Princess Hildegarde. What sort of hocus pocus did he plan that would cause Mr. Samuel Wyche to appear and the Princess Hildegarde to disappear at one and the same time? Or was this merely another of his devious schemes?

Chapter 17

"I fully intend to accompany you and Celeste when you call on the prince," Mrs. Gordon told her daughter early the next afternoon as they finished their luncheon in the dining room. "Furthermore, I shall go on with you to meet the prince's uncle, King Harlan. Nothing you say will deter me; I am quite determined."

"I fail to understand why you wish to come," Rowena protested, "since you've objected to the prince from the first."

"Objected for very good and sufficient reasons. However, when a young man proclaims his intention to marry my only daughter, without, I may add, seeking her mother's consent beforehand, I believe I have not only the right but the duty to meet him and make my opinions known regarding the suitability of the match. And I shall. Fortunately, the friend I visited in Brighton returned to town with me and so I shall be here indefinitely."

"I have no doubt Lothar will seek your consent,

mama. Everything happened so quickly."

"And whose doing was that? Running off to my sister in the country indeed!"

"Rowena had every reason to be upset," Celeste said. "She was in desperate need of comfort."

"A sensible course would have been to ask me to return to London. I would have, in a trice." Mrs. Gordon smiled, rather sadly, Celeste thought. "However," she went on, "I realize your objections to my meeting the prince and his uncle are not so much because of my feelings toward the prince, which are, by the bye, much less hostile now than you may imagine. To be blunt, Rowena, you fear I may either embarrass you by doing something terribly *gauche* or create a frightful scene."

Rowena lowered her head. "No, mama, surely not," she said although Celeste knew this was exactly what she did fear.

"I am not unacquainted with royalty," Mrs. Gordon said, "having known members of European royal houses both formally and somewhat—what shall I say?—informally. And not royalty from some obscure hyphenated kingdom, either."

Rowena, obviously made uncomfortable by her mother's veiled allusions, glanced at the long clock. "We should be on our way," she said.

"Our carriage is waiting." Mrs. Gordon led them into the front hall and, as she put on her hat, proceeded to examine her daughter from toe to crown. Her eyes narrowed.

Celeste was aware that Rowena had vacillated endlessly in selecting her gown, finally choosing a shiny percale in bishop's blue with long puffed sleeves. A large yellow bow bloomed at the waist with a smaller matching bow below the square decolletage; three tiers of yellow ruffles decorated the gown just above the hem. She wore a fichu of pale yellow, blue gloves and a hat plumed with yellow and blue feathers.

The gown, Celeste thought, all the mode though it might be, was overly fussy, but she had hesitated to disapprove of Rowena's choice. Now she regretted her silence since, to put not too fine a point on it, the gown quite overwhelmed Rowena. Mrs. Gordon also seemed to harbor doubts but, after a glance at the clock, merely frowned before leading the way to the carriage.

They arrived at the prince's lodgings on Blenheim Street shortly after two. Lothar, again wearing his captain's uniform, greeted them warmly and, although he took pains to appear to be in great good humor, Celeste detected an underlying unease. She felt it was no wonder he seemed perturbed since he could only look forward to a stormy reception from his uncle later in the afternoon.

Roderic had not yet made his promised appearance, leaving Celeste both disappointed and relieved. Her keen desire to see him and to be with him had not abated and yet she wondered if his newfound enthusiasm for the match between the prince and Rowena would prove to be sincere. More importantly, his doubts concerning their own suitability, one for the other, had sown and nurtured doubts in her mind. Their differences created a chasm almost impossible to bridge even with the best of intentions on both their parts. Perhaps, she decided, it would be best for all concerned if he failed to appear.

They had barely settled themselves, however, when Roderic was announced. He strode into the room exuding confidence, saluting Lothar and bowing over the three ladies' hands.

"I took the liberty," Roderic said to Lothar, "of inviting a guest."

Celeste held her breath apprehensively as he returned to the doorway to murmur a few words to someone in the entry hall. When he again entered the room he was escorting a strikingly beautiful golden-haired young lady who carried herself with an air of elegance. At first glance her green gown seemed no more than gracefully simple but Celeste, noting the clever cut and the expensive material, realized it must have cost an extravagant amount.

"Allow me to introduce," Roderic said, "the Princess Hildegarde."

They all stared at the blue-eyed princess, Lothar in the stunned surprise befitting a gentleman who finds himself in the same room with his two fiancées at the same time, Rowena with a look of sickened despair and Mrs. Gordon with an "I-expected-this-all-along" expression on her face. Celeste, once her initial shock ebbed, glared at Roderic and was not surprised when he refused to meet her gaze.

Roderic led the princess across the room and presented her to Lothar. "The princess is newly arrived from Paris," he told him.

Lothar, still at a loss for words, blinked and then sketched a bow. As he did, Celeste hurried to Rowena's side and clasped her friend's hand. Rowena's cold fingers closed on hers in a grip of desperation.

"How handsome a figure you are in your uniform," the princess told Lothar in slightly accented English. "I never imagined to find my betrothed such a dashing officer of the guard."

And how tall and regal the princess was, Celeste thought. For some reason she had pictured her as being plump and dowdy, perhaps because years before the Prince Regent's German bride-to-be had proved to be such a disappointment. Such was not the case at all, for the Princess Hildegarde was as beautiful and as graceful as a swan. Almost any man, Celeste suspected, would find her captivating.

Lothar shifted uncomfortably from foot to foot, saying nothing.

"How surprised I was to receive a letter from Lord Campion offering to bring me to London," the princess said. "Since our funds are somewhat less than plentiful, we accepted at once."

"We?" Lothar asked. "You and your entourage?"

Roderic cleared his throat. "It so happens that the Princess Hildegarde is married," he said, "and has been for more than a year. I had the great good pleasure of meeting her husband yesterday."

Celeste heard Rowena gasp and felt her friend's hand tighten on hers.

"My husband is the Comte de Montalbert." The princess said the name with evident pride. "He is acquainted with many of the émigres who sought and found refuge in England during the Terror of the nineties. It was most kind of Lord Campion to offer both of us the opportunity to visit them."

"You should have told us the princess was married," Celeste protested to Roderic, her relief mingling with anger. "How unfair of you to keep silent."

"Why the devil didn't you?" Lothar demanded.

Roderic extended his arms, palms out, in a placating gesture. "It was impossible for me to resist creating this moment of high drama," he said. "In my defense, I ask you to consider this. If I had never written to the princess, do you realize how much time might have passed before all of us learned the truth? I should be thanked for removing this obstacle to the happiness of Lothar and Rowena, not rebuked for my manner of revealing the truth."

"Your success was quite inadvertant," Celeste told him, "and did not come about because you have a sensible and feeling mind."

He was so glib, so very sure of himself! And yet she felt her initial cold fury melting to mere annoyance. How easy it was for her to forgive him his deceptions. In fact, to forgive him almost anything.

"I expected you to be quite different," the princess admitted to Lothar. "I pictured a huge blustering young man with enormous moustaches. A man with a narrow mind and a cold heart."

"And I thought of you as being frumpy and rather plump. I must admit I was very wrong."

"If we had met a few years ago," the princess said softly, "what a different course our lives might have followed. But such is fate, is that not so?"

Rowena went to stand at Lothar's side, clasping his hand and holding it possessively against her side. "The prince and I are betrothed," she said.

The princess looked at her for a long moment during which Celeste thought she detected a slight rising of her regal eyebrows. "So Lord Campion said to me." The princess hesitated before adding, "May you both find the serenity and happiness you deserve."

"Thank you," Rowena said coolly.

"And now I must bid you all farewell," the princess said. "The comte awaits my return and the comte is an impatient man." Accepting Lord Campion's offer to escort her to her carriage, she glided from the room, leaving behind a faint, pleasing scent and the lingering memory that beauty evokes.

Before Roderic returned and while the prince and Mrs. Gordon were remarking on the sudden appearance of the princess and her startling news, Celeste noticed Rowena leave the prince's side to stand before a large oval looking glass. Evidently she was not pleased with what she saw there, for when she turned away her expression showed a worried dissatisfaction as she nervously fingered the large bow at her waist.

"I had expected Mr. Samuel Wyche to have arrived by this time," Roderic said. "As you see, he has not appeared as yet."

"Ah, the elusive Mr. Wyche." Lothar shook his head sadly. "What a fool I was to place my trust in that glib scoundrel; I should have recognized his glowing vision of wealth for the foolish fancy it turned out to be. I learned my lesson, bitter though it was. I promise that never again will I place at risk as much as a single guinea that I can ill afford to lose."

"Speaking as someone with slightly more experience than you, my dear prince," Mrs. Gordon said, "resolutions to change one's character are easy to make but difficuilt to put into practice."

"Perhaps. But whenever I might be tempted to speculate in land or anything else, I shall remember Mr. Samuel Wyche and his alchemist's vision of earth transformed into gold."

"And if you fail to remember him," Rowena promised, "I shall most certainly remind you."

"Excellent," Roderic said with a self-satisfied smile, "this is precisely the result I envisioned from the very beginning."

Not at all certain what he was congratulating himself for, Celeste challenged him. "And what, pray tell," she asked, "does that signify?"

"King Harlan warned me of Lothar's profligate habits and I had occasion to observe them myself at the gaming tables. I found him to be exceedingly reckless, shockingly so. Therefore I sought out Mr. Samuel Wyche, a gentleman I admit possesses a rather shady reputation, and he directed my attention to the property offered for sale near the Regent's Park. How beguiled Lothar would be, I told myself."

"Thank you very much," Lothar said, meaning quite the opposite. "So you then proceeded to turn your Mr. Wyche loose on me."

"For your own good, my friend. Though Mr. Wyche solicited your funds, I assure you he never purchased so much as a square foot of that country land. Your money is quite safe; Mr. Wyche will arrive directly and return it to you with every pence, shilling and guinea intact."

Roderic must imagine himself to be frightfully clever, Rowena thought even as she sighed in relief at the prince's good fortune. Why must he employ these dubious schemes? Why does he find it so difficult to be straightforward?

"Should I thank you for saving me from myself?" Lothar asked. "Or should I take offense at this trickery of yours?"

"Thank him," Rowena said. "Now, no matter whether your uncle disinherits you or not, we at least have more than a few shillings to our name."

"Heed her, Lothar," Roderic said. "You should be grateful to me rather than condemn me. When a surgeon discovers a disease that threatens to become mortal, as did your gambling, immediate and decisive action is required to save the patient."

Celeste did *not* approve. Roderic had been blatantly dishonest even though his ploy seemed to have succeeded. "Can you trust your Mr. Wyche to appear here today?" she asked. "After all, he may have seen fit to abscond with the prince's money. You yourself admit his reputation is less than admirable."

"Mr. Wyche will appear. He would never make off with the money; his money-making ways are more devious. Never fear, I understand the likes of Wyche."

Lothar's manservant appeared in the doorway. "Mr. Samuel Wyche," he announced.

"Ah," Roderic said with a smile, "Mr. Wyche has come to us as I promised you he would."

Mr. Samuel Wyche, stumpy and florid, his broad-brimmed black hat held at his side, entered the room nodding and bowing to right and left. To Celeste, he appeared perturbed and wary.

Roderic clasped his hand. "I have this minute told my friends the details of our little ploy," he said. "If you would be so kind as to return the prince's investment, we shall have an end to the matter to the satisfaction of all."

Mr. Wyche shifted his hat from hand to hand, glancing at Roderic and then at the prince, his gaze finally becoming fixed on a two-edged sword displayed above the mantel. "All will be for the best," he said with none of his usual enthusiasm. "Have no doubt of that."

"Exactly so." Roderic frowned impatiently. "Such will be the case as soon as the prince has his money in hand."

Mr. Wyche raised and lowered his shoulders in a massive sigh. Facing Roderic, his studied diction and his composure fleeing at one and the same time, he blurted, "I ain't got the money, your lordship."

Roderic took a step toward him. "What's that you say?" he asked.

"'Twas this way," Wyche said, almost tearfully. "I was so taken by the prospects of the land at Regent's Park I used the prince's ready with all the spare I had to my name and bought it."

Agape, Roderic stared at him. "You . . . bought . . . the . . . land?"

Mr. Wyche thrust his hand into an inside pocket of his black coat, bringing forth and unrolling a document replete with gold seals and red ribbons. "The deed to the land," he said. Scrabbling in another pocket, he produced yet another paper. "The bill of sale."

Roderic snatched the documents from him and perused them. "By God," he said, "the scoundrel's telling the truth. All of Lothar's money and some of his own have gone into the purchase of land."

"It appears Mr. Wyche," Celeste said caustically, "was so convincing when he extolled the merits of the speculation that he convinced himself. And succeeded in becoming one of his own victims."

Roderic, still staring in disbelief first at one of the documents and then the other, shook his head.

"Mr. Wyche must wait for later," Lothar said with an uneasy glance at the clock. "The hour is late and the King awaits us." He held out his hand to Rowena. "We shall face the king together," he said, "and learn our fate."

Chapter 18

"You must go on without me to meet the King," Rowena said to Lothar as they stood on the walkway in front of his lodgings. "I intend to follow after first stopping at our house." She turned to her mother. "Mama, will you please come with me?"

"Of course," Mrs. Gordon told her.

"You *will* return to meet the King?" Lothar asked with an edge of uncertainty in his voice. "You have naught to fear from my uncle since he has no quarrel with you, Rowena, only with me."

"I promise to join you," she said, "and very soon."

After Rowena and her mother departed, Lothar, Roderic and Celeste drove to the residence of the Marien-Holstein ambassador on Whitecross Street where King Harlan, garbed in a red and orange Marshal of the Army uniform, greeted them in one of the reception chambers, a dark cramped room with elaborate chandeliers suspended from a high ceiling, a room where somber portraits gazed down from the walls at them in disapproval, a room as small and every bit as ill-situated as the kingdom of Marien-Holstein itself.

The king bowed over Celeste's hand, embraced his nephew and shook hands with Roderic. When he said, "Jolly good to see you," Celeste recalled being told he had learned English from a former member of the *ton* who had fled the country to avoid being imprisoned for failure to pay his debts.

"Miss Gordon and her mother will join us anon," Lothar told him.

"Capital!" the king cried even as his face clouded over with displeasure. Celeste groaned inwardly; if the mere mention of the Gordon name perturbed him, what chance did Rowena have?

In reply to Lothar's question, the king assured them that his wife, the queen, remained in good health and excellent spirits. Since it appeared certain that the naval treaty would never be signed, he added dolefully, he meant to return to her side in the very near future.

"The Princess from Stuttgart," Roderic said, "the Princess Hildegarde, Lothar's betrothed, is in London. His former betrothed, I might add, for we discovered she is married to another."

The king raised his eyebrows but then shrugged as though the news had little significance. He was determined, Celeste realized, to oppose his nephew's match and no amount of persuasion or argument could possibly sway him.

An awkward silence was broken when the king said to Roderic, "By Jove, Campion, I must congratulate you."

"On the marriage of the Princess Hildegarde?"

"No, no, on your great success."

Roderic appeared nonplused. "For the most part," he admitted, "I failed to accomplish anything."

"In one important matter," the King told him, "one we did not discuss when last we met, you were top of the trees, truly a paragon. I refer, of course, to the merchandising or Mr. Roemermann's fine soap."

"His soap?" Roderic echoed, scowling.

Celeste smiled to herself, recalling how nettled he had been when first Mrs. Atkinson and then Mr. Hugh B. Garson had twitted him for becoming a peddler of soap.

"The sales of Roemermann Soap in the Belvedere Shops and elsewhere in England have been more than up to snuff," the King said proudly. "Our soap works are busy day and night and Mr. Roemermann is at this moment erecting a monstrous new building to permit him to increase his production threefold. Money pours into Marien-Holstein in exchange for our nonesuch soap. This, my dear Roderic, is all your doing. We are grateful; you have every reason to be high in the instep."

"I *am* proud of being able to help your country." Roderic bowed his acknowledgement of the king's accolade while Celeste felt a glow of pleasure at his unexpected triumph.

"Marien-Holstein," the king told him, "will present you with our Legion of Merit, the highest award given to a foreigner. I hereby invite you to travel to Marienhaven in the near future to receive this great honor."

"I promise to come," Roderic told him. "And I am honored. And undeserving, since I did nothing more than make gifts of the soap to a few of my friends. Any honors should go to Mr. Roemermann."

The king waved aside his modest disclaimer. "Pray permit me to tell you more of Mr. Roemermann," he said. "You will find this very interesting. And frightfully romantic. Mr. Roemermann is a dab hand with soap but not, I fear, with the ladies. He is, in fact, a bachelor who has spent most of his life either in his laboratory creating better soaps or amidst his bubbling vats producing those soaps.

"Two months ago he had occasion to engage a room at a hotel in Marienhaven, the same hotel, by the bye, where you, my dear Roderic, stayed when you visited my country this past winter. Mr. Roemermann had forgotten to bring his own supply of soap with him—he habitually does, I understand—and so, rather than use the inferior product the hotel provided, went in search of some. And this is where a benevolent fate intervened."

Roderic raised his hand. "Pray allow me to attempt to foretell what happened next, your majesty." He lowered his head and closed his eyes, placing his hand to his forehead as though deep in thought. "Ah," he said when he opened his eyes, "here is what I see: Mr. Roemermann, in his search for a cake of his own soap, met the daughter of the establishment and, overwhelmed by her modest charm as well as her good sense in giving him his own superior product, offered for her hand and, in due course, was accepted."

"Just so!" the king exclaimed. Obviously puzzled, he stared at Roderic. "Since I only heard the good news as I was setting sail for London, by what legerdemain did you discover the truth?"

Yes, Celeste thought, how did Roderic know? Legerdemain, she strongly suspected, had nothing at all to do with it.

"If you recall," Roderic said, "I never explained how I accomplished my coup on the Exchange following the Battle of Waterloo. Likewise, I am unfortunately not at liberty to reveal my source of information, not even to you, your majesty."

The king was starting to protest when he noticed his manservant standing in the doorway trying to catch his eye. He gave him his royal acknowledgement.

"Mrs. Jane Gordon," the servant announced, "and Miss Rowena Gordon."

Lothar hastened to the doorway, nodded to Mrs. Gordon, murmured a few words to Rowena and offered her his arm. As Rowena crossed the room, Celeste drew in her breath, a thrill of pleased surprise rushing through her.

Rowena was transformed. She now wore an elegantly simple white silk gown that shimmered as she walked. A single strand of pearls circled her neck, and her black ringlets were held in place by a pearl diadem. The change, though, was not so much in Rowena's apparel—she herself seemed different. She glowed, she walked with grace and confidence, she possessed an air of almost regal self-assurance.

Celeste was unable to decide whether this metamorphosis had been brought about by the prince's avowal of everlasting love—how powerful that sweet emotion could be!—or by the example of the Princess Hildegarde or by the discovery of some inner strength of her own laying dormant until called forth in this, her hour of trial. Whatever the cause, the change had occurred and a glance at the others in the room told Celeste that they, too, had been struck by it.

Rowena had become a princess.

Celeste felt a welling of pride on behalf of her friend. No matter what the King might decree, Rowena would never be the same again; she had triumphed. Along with her joy, Celeste experienced a twinge of loss, realizing that she and Rowena could never be as close to one another in the future as they had been in the past. Does a princess come to one's bedchamber to share her hopes and dreams? Does a princess frolic in the snow?

Mrs. Gordon curtsied and Rowena followed suit; the King bowed over their hands. Before anyone could speak, Lothar stepped forward. "I must inform you I have offered for Miss Gordon's hand," he told his uncle, the ring of a challenge in his voice, "and she has done me the honor of accepting."

"This is neither the time nor the place to—" the King began.

Roderic interrupted. "If your majesty will allow me to speak," he said.

The King glared at him. "You already have spoken without my permission, Lord Campion."

"When I returned to London from Marien-Holstein," Roderic said, ignoring the rebuke, "I was convinced that the proposed alliance between the prince and Miss Gordon should be opposed and, as both Lothar and Miss Prescott will testify, I did all in my power to thwart it. Without success. I have, though, changed my mind and beg you, your majesty, to do the same."

"And what, pray tell, brought about this sudden change of heart? Sentiment?"

"Yes, in part." As the king shook his head, seemingly in disappointment at Roderic's poor judgment, Roderic went on to explain. "But only in part. I firmly believe a prince who marries for love will become a better ruler than one who weds merely for political or other reasons. As you know, our own Prince Regent married a German princess against his own inclinations. The marriage is conceded to be an unhappy one and of late the Regent has come to be universally reviled for his excesses."

"A young man in the throes of love," the king said, "is like a loose screw, and more often than not chooses unwisely. A love match with an unsuitable partner is doomed."

"Perhaps. Yet who among us has the temerity to judge who is or is not suitable?" The king seemed about to raise an objection only to have Roderic plunge on. "In a place of honor in the Gordon drawing room," he said, "is a portrait of General Gordon, the father of Mrs. Jane Gordon." He nodded toward Rowena's mother. "My research into the family uncovered an extremely pertinent fact about the general."

"And that fact is?" the King asked.

"One of the great disappointments of his life was his repeated failure to sire a male heir to carry on the Gordon name and military tradition. He became the father, to his everlasting chagrin, of one female after another. He had a grand total of not two or three daughters, your majesty, but seven!"

"Ahhh," King Harlan said. Celeste imagined him picturing the daughters of Lothar and Rowena marrying into most of the royal houses of Europe and thus assuring the existence of Marien-Holstein.

"In addition to which," Roderic said, "these daughters to date have themselves been the proud mothers of nine children and eight of these nine children were also daughters. Can such a circumstance be mere chance? I think not. How this might apply to the prince is, of course, a rather delicate subject not to be discussed with ladies present so I intend to refrain from speculating further. I expect, however, your majesty understands the thrust of my argument."

"By Jove, I do, Roderic, I do. And yet, when placed onto the balance I fear such a wicked number of daughters fails to tip the scales in favor of the match. There is so much on the other side of the ledger."

Before Roderic could answer, Mrs. Gordon said, "May I speak, your majesty?"

The King scowled but said, "Pray do," in his most uninviting tone of voice.

Celeste stared at Rowena's mother, perturbed by the fear that whatever Mrs. Gordon might say would tip the king's scales (or unbalance his ledger, depending on which metaphor he favored at the moment) even more against Rowena. There was, however, nothing she could do to stop Mrs. Gordon from speaking her mind.

"I have every reason to believe," Mrs. Gordon said, "that in your majesty's mind, *my* actions rather than those of my daughter are weighing against this marriage."

When the king, looking desperately uncomfortable, said neither yea nor nay to the charge, Rowena put a restraining hand on her mother's sleeve but Mrs. Gordon ignored her plea for silence.

"At first," Mrs. Gordon said, "I must admit I opposed the prince's attentions to my daughter. The reports I received pictured his character as less than exemplary, making him unsuitable for a young and rather naive young lady such as Rowena. Your nephew, or so I believed then, simply would not do."

"Lothar is a prince," the king said as if that fact excused anything and everything.

"Be that as it may—there are princes and then again there are princes—I soon reconsidered my opposition at the urging of my daughter and Miss Prescott. Now I favor the match although you, your majesty, have made it quite evident that you do not."

"True enough," the king said, "and you, my dear lady, are very much mistaken if you expect me to change my opinion after listening to your pleas. No matter how impassioned they may become. Or how tearful."

"Is that all you expect from women, your majesty? Either passion or tears? In this case, neither is called for. I suspect the application of pure logic will suffice to change your mind."

"Pure logic, Mrs. Gordon? I have yet to meet a logical woman but I will hear you out."

"I happen to have a dear friend who has offered to speak for me, a gentleman who has been waiting in your drafty antechamber ever since my daughter and I arrived. If you would be good enough to call for him."

The king rang, bidding his servant to fetch the gentleman in question, and after a few minutes the servant returned and announced, "Lord Howell, Earl of Broadmoor."

"Lord Howell!" Lothar and Roderic exclaimed in unison as a ginger-haired, ginger-bearded gentleman of a certain age—Celeste judged him to be twenty years older than Mrs. Gordon—entered the room. Lothar hastened to the king's side and whispered in his ear.

So this was the elusive Lord Howell, Celeste thought, the man who had the power to either recommend or scuttle the naval treaty. How very bluff and ordinary he looked, although his green eyes, she noted, glittered shrewdly.

Lord Howell acknowledged everyone with brief nods before bowing stiffly to the king.

"My nephew, Prince Lothar," the king said, "informs me he has discussed the Marien-Holstein naval treaty with you. With scant success."

"Holiday at Brighton," Lord Howell explained. "Man needs his holidays to rejuvenate, not for work."

The king glanced at Mrs. Gordon and then looked back at Lord Howell, seemingly unsure how to proceed. "Perhaps," he suggested, "we two should have a private conversation regarding the naval treaty."

"No need. No secrets. All open and aboveboard, that's my motto. Always has been."

"The naval treaty is of tremendous importance to me and to my country—" the King began.

Lord Howell shook his head. "Know all that," he

said. "No need to talk details, it's either aye or nay to my way of thinking." He nodded toward Rowena. "Now then," he said, "they tell me this English girl's not good enough for this high and mighty prince of yours."

"No one has said that, Lord Howell." The king looked around the room. "Has anyone said that?"

"And no one will?" Lord Howell asked. "Not now? Not ever?"

"In your mind," the king said, "the naval treaty and the marriage are linked? Are you suggesting—?"

"Suggesting? Suggesting nothing, nothing at all. Not my decision whether to sign your damned treaty, the Navy Board decides all that. I recommend, they decide. As for me, I make up my own mind. No one sways me, no one at all. Is that not the case, Jane?"

Mrs. Gordon nodded her agreement. "Lord Howell has always made his decisions following a thorough study of the subject at hand and after judiciously weighing all the pros and cons. Since Lord Howell is highly respected for his integrity and good sense, his recommendations are almost always followed by the Navy Board."

"Just so," Lord Howell said. "Couldn't put it better myself. Exactly."

The king put his hand to his chin as he pondered the implications of what he had heard. "The kingdom of Marien-Holstein," he said, "would be honored to have one of the members of its royal family marry a young English lady, particularly one as handsome and amiable as Miss Rowena Gordon."

Celeste barely controlled her cry of elation. Rowena ran to Lothar, hugging him, then went to

Lord Howell and kissed him on the cheek. As Lord Howell beamed, Celeste turned to the king and, after she curtsied gracefully, the king reached for her hand and helped her rise.

During the round of congratulations and best wishes that followed, Celeste noticed that Roderic stood to one side, saying little.

The king quickly settled the details, occasionally asking for Lothar's advice and, less often, taking it. The royal wedding would be in Marienhaven three months hence, in June, he decided, with, besides her mother, all of Rowena's aunts invited. He and the prince would return to Marien-Holstein at once to oversee the preparations while Rowena would remain in London with her mother. Celeste gladly accepted Rowena's invitation to stay at the Gordon's with the proviso that she would also spend a few days visiting her cousin, Miss Lola Argent. Celeste had no notion what she would do following the wedding.

"And you, Roderic," the king asked, "what are your plans?"

"I intend to visit my mother," he said. "After several weeks with her in the Lake District I shall sail for Marien-Holstein to receive your much appreciated though little deserved award and, of course, attend the wedding."

Celeste bit her lip as she tried not to reveal her feelings. Even though she had expected Roderic to leave London, to leave her, his terse declaration dismayed her. True, they were unsuitable, not only because of social position but also, and perhaps more important to him, temperament. And yet her heart told her she would never love another man as she loved Roderic Courtney-Trench. No, not Roderic, she told herself ruefully. He must be Lord Campion to her from now on.

After saying their farewells to the king, they left the ambassador's residence together. Lothar and Rowena again thanked Lord Howell for his timely intervention, then dallied over their goodbyes while Celeste walked ahead with Rowena's mother to the Gordon carriage.

"Miss Prescott," Lord Campion called to her.

Miss Prescott. Even though she had anticipated the formality of his words, she winced. Drawing in a deep breath to quell her agitation, she waited while Lord Howell handed Mrs. Gordon into the carriage and then turned to Lord Campion.

He raised her gloved hand to his lips, holding her hand in his as he looked at her, saying nothing, his face strained and unhappy. Or was she mistakenly assigning her own emotions to him? Or was that how she wanted him to feel, expected him to feel? Though she doubted it was the case, she hoped his heart was breaking, as hers most decidedly was.

For a long moment, as her gaze met and held his, the sights and sounds of the city seemed to fade until the two of them were alone together in a world of their own, to her, as always, a truly magical world where, if she could but wish it so, they would dwell forever.

How handsome he was in his purple waistcoat, white cravat and grey trousers! His head was bare—he held his grey hat in his hand—and when she saw that the breeze had sent strands of his dark hair curling in disarray onto his forehead, she had to resist an impulse to push them back into place. His brown eyes, those unique eyes with their small gold wedges mesmerized her as his gaze wandered from her head to her toe as though he meant to memorize each and every aspect of her.

Because, she reminded herself, he meant to leave her, never to return.

This drear realization jolted Celeste from her trance and she withdrew her hand from his. He started to speak, or so she thought, but stopped, all the while keeping his gaze on her. She vowed she would not be the first to look away and at last, with a sigh, he murmured "Goodbye," his voice husky, and, not waiting for her reply, swung away from her and strode to Lothar's waiting landau.

He climbed into the carriage without looking back. Although Celeste's vision was misted by tears, she could see well enough to tell that when the carriage turned from Whitecross Street and disappeared from her view he was still staring straight ahead.

Chapter 19

Roderic and Lothar walked slowly along the rocky beach in their black greatcoats, scarves wrapped about their necks, their heads lowered against the chill wind sweeping in off the North Sea. A single gull took flight ahead of them, mewing as it rose into the grey, lowering sky. To their right, a half mile out to sea, a three-masted ship bound for London from Marienhaven sailed slowly westward through angry white-capped waves.

"I bring you good news from London," Roderic said.

"You look decidedly glum for a bearer of good news."

"After the bustle of London," Roderic admitted, "the Lake District seemed rather dull even though I found my mother in good health and busy with her garden and her societies for the betterment of womankind. Of course she also enjoys attempting to improve me, which I find somewhat tedious."

"Mothers always see room for improvement,"

Lothar said with a wry smile.

Roderic nodded as he led the way inland from the shore toward a grove of windswept trees. "But let me tell you the good news, news made all the better by being completely unexpected. None other than Mr. Samuel Wyche informed me that he had received an offer for your land holdings near the Regent's Park, an offer fifty percent above the price you paid. Since Wyche's honesty leaves a bit to be desired, I went to considerable trouble to confirm his claim and found there is such an offer, a legitimate one to boot."

"Capital! And what does our Mr. Wyche intend to do with his portion?"

"As you might expect, he means to sell at once. Mr. Wyche invariably seeks a quick return on his funds. He said something about wanting to purchase a volume of memoirs."

They paused when they reached the shelter of the grove, sitting side by side on the trunk of a fallen tree.

"For my part," Lothar said, "I shall not sell. How many Londoners are there today? A million? In seventy-five or a hundred years there may well be twice that number, each and every one requiring a place to live. I intend to keep the land and pass it on to my children or my grandchildren. This little enclave of ours, this kingdom of Marien-Holstein, may not survive another hundred years, but England will. And London will. Do you agree with my decision, Roderic?"

When his friend made no reply, Lothar leaned toward him, snapping his fingers and smiling when Roderic blinked into awareness. "Roderic?" he asked.

"Sorry, my thoughts were far from here."

"May I hazard a guess as to precisely where they were? I would say they were to be found in London but not with our Mr. Wyche. Could it be they dwell on a certain charming young lady?"

Roderic rose and paced back and forth in front of Lothar, his hands clasped behind his back. "Damn, damn, damn," he said. "This is not good, not good at all."

"Then why in the name of heaven do you procrastinate? Especially when both of us realize what you must do to bring an end to your self-inflicted pain."

Roderic struck his open palm with his fist. "I have a desperate need only she can satisfy," he said. "I should do it. I must do it. I shall do it. Give me your best wishes, Lothar. When she arrives for your wedding in June, I intend to offer for her."

Lothar sprang to his feet, shook his friend's hand and embraced him. "Why have you waited so long?" he asked.

"Long? When did I meet her? A few months ago, no more, and a few months is hardly an inordinately long time." He hesitated before going on. "Her lack of a dowry, her lack of a place in society, they mean nothing to me. The difference in temperaments, ah, there's the only rub."

"I find her exceedingly amiable. Besides which, she possesses a sharp mind and is honest to a fault."

"Just so, to a fault. And often that honesty grates since she chides me every time I attempt the slightest ruse, accusing me of being a deceitful schemer. If she does that now, what the devil will she be like in ten years?" He threw up his hands. "But I have no choice, not the slightest. Life without her is unbearable."

"You could change, Roderic, become more like her."

"I intend to try to be more forthright, yet I can only promise her improvement, not the perfection she seeks. Women make a habit of expecting the impossible from men."

"I suggest you write immediately to inform her of your sentiments."

"No, words put on paper have a nasty way of betraying one, of being misread. I must ask for her hand while we are face to face. I say this even though at this very moment I can picture her sitting in the Gordon drawing room, bereft."

Lothar raised his eyebrows. "Your imaginings may well be correct, since in a letter Rowena wrote a fortnight ago—she writes me daily though the letters arrive not singly but in clusters—she mentions that Celeste recently acquired a dog as a companion."

"A dog? What sort of dog? She did refer once to a liking for dogs. On that day we visited Mr. Hugh B. Garson, I believe it was."

"She now is the owner of a small brown spaniel. It must be to assuage her loneliness."

Roderic's expression became thoughtful. "That," he said finally, "is undoubtedly the reason."

Several days later Roderic walked to the palace to visit his friend, finding him in the music room making selections for his wedding. Roderic sat at the pianoforte and began to play.

"A pleasant melody," Lothar said when he finished.

"That was the Haydn sonata Celeste played at Mrs. Gordon's musical evening." He swung sideways on the bench to face Lothar. "Have you received more letters from Rowena?"

"I have indeed. She writes that both the weather and the shopping in London are delightful; her mother is in splendid health and sends her love; and her aunts are agog, one and all, over the prospect of journeying to Marien-Holstein next month for the wedding."

"What of Celeste Prescott? Have you no word of her?"

"Rowena did tell me that Celeste had left the Gordon house to spend the next week or so with her cousin, a Miss Ardent."

"Not Ardent, Miss Lola Argent. Is that all?"

"Give me a moment to recall. Oh yes, Rowena did mention she and Celeste had driven to Hyde Park, where they had a pleasant time frolicking with the dogs."

"The dogs? What dogs? I understood Celeste had but one dog, a spaniel."

Lothar knitted his brow. "Pray let me try to remember," he said. "I believe Rowena mentioned two other dogs, both Irish setters. It seems Celeste and her cousin, Miss Argent, are in the habit of walking them in the park. They could be Miss Argent's dogs. Or Celeste may have reasoned that if one dog would ease her heartache over your absence, three dogs would ease it threefold."

Roderic struck a series of discordant notes on the piano. "These attempts at humor, Lothar," he said, "are neither comical nor appreciated." He scowled. "If I were granted three wishes by a genie, my first would be to have Mr. Hugh B. Garson change into a dog forthwith, becoming a mongrel of some indeterminate breed. If he did, both he and I would be much happier."

"The question, however, is whether Celeste would be. I believe I suggested you write to her. Did you?"

Roderic shook his head. "Nothing untoward will happen in London before she sails for Marienhaven. Nothing."

"For your sake, Roderic," Lothar said, "I hope you've not miscalculated." He failed to add "again," but the word hung in the air between them.

On a Saturday afternoon in May, Roderic Courtney-Trench received the Legion of Merit from King Harlan for "his unstinting and exemplary services to the Kingdom of Marien-Holstein."

At the reception that followed the ceremony, Roderic took the first opportunity to seek out Prince Lothar. "Congratulations," Lothar said, warmly shaking his friend's hand.

"A most impressive ceremony." Roderic's halfhearted tone showed that something other than the award was on his mind. "Have you received any word from London?" he asked anxiously.

"You really should have written to Celeste. Or allowed me to say something of your intentions to Rowena."

"Tell me the news at once, Lothar. What is it? What have you heard that you hesitate to report?"

"I received a letter from Rowena this morning, a letter she wrote more than a week ago. She saw Celeste driving in Hyde Park in an elegant carriage. Not alone. She was accompanied by a gentleman."

"Did she say who this gentleman was?"

"Unfortunately, she failed to see his face. She noticed, however, two rather large wolfhounds riding in the carriage with Celeste and the gentleman."

"Good God! I feared as much. Mr. Hugh B. Garson. There can be no doubt of it."

"When next she visited Celeste at her cousin's, Rowena questioned her, in an indirect and courteous manner, of course, but found her answers evasive, neither revealing a growing tenderness for someone nor denying such an emotion."

"This is absolutely unbelievable. All those damnable dogs. I really believed Celeste possessed more sense. I quite give her up."

"I must make you aware of one more ominous omen," Lothar said. "Rowena writes that Celeste has told her that circumstances beyond her control may prevent her from attending our wedding next month. Celeste gave no reason nor did Rowena speculate in her letter, she merely stated the fact."

"This is more than too much, Lothar." Roderic clapped his friend on the shoulder. "Pray wish me godspeed," he said, "since I depart for London on the next ship that sails from Marienhaven."

Roderic reached London early on a Friday morning and, hiring a hackney cab, proceeded without delay to the Gordon townhouse. After what he considered an inordinately long wait in the drawing room under the watchful eye of General Gordon, Rowena appeared, exclaiming over his unexpected arrival in England.

"Have you word of Celeste?" he demanded without pausing for any of the customary civilities.

She frowned and shook her head. "Not for several days," she told him. "As I wrote Lothar, she seems much preoccupied of late."

"For God's sake," he said, "tell me where this cousin of hers, this Miss Argent, lives."

She unhesitatingly supplied him with the directions and, after a hasty goodbye, he hurried off in the hackney.Miss Argent herself answered his peremptory knocking on her door. After identifying himself, he inquired, with as much calm as he could muster, after Celeste.

Miss Argent at once became all adither. "She left in a travelling carriage this very morning," she said. "I was quite flabbergasted. More than a person can stand, all these upheavals, all this coming and going, especially when one is afflicted, as I happen to be, with the Argent nerves."

Roderic groaned. "Have you any notion where she went?" he asked. "Any notion at all?"

"Where do romantically inclined young people go nowadays when they run off with unseemly haste? To Scotland, I expect. To Gretna Green."

"Good God! I feared as much. Who was he, this man she was with?"

"I never once caught sight of the gentleman. All I can say for certain is there were two hounds barking from his carriage windows."

"Just as I suspected. Hugh B. Garson. How long ago did they leave?"

"Not over an hour has passed since their carriage departed," Miss Argent told him.

Roderic nodded his thanks and hurried down the stairs.

Ordering the hackney driver to stop at a livery, he hired a bay gelding and set off at a gallop for the north, passing through the tollgates and finally leaving the stones behind. Since they had no suspicion they were being pursued, he could overtake them, he assured himself. He must overtake them. What a fool he was to have delayed offering for her.

Suppressing his roiling panic, he rode on between newly sown fields, crested a hill and saw, less than a half mile ahead, a carriage no different from many others except for the wolfhound with its grey head thrusting from an open window. Urging his horse to greater speed, Rowena soon drew alongside, hailed the driver and ordered him to halt. To his pleased surprise, the carriage slowed to a stop at the side of the road.

Roderic swung from his horse, strode to the carriage and flung open the door. Both dogs barked; one plunged past him and ran across the road and back again but gave no sign of any hostile intent. Peering into the dim interior of the carriage he saw Celeste—how lovely and desirable she looked—with the other dog sitting at her feet eyeing him warily and growling. Hugh B. Garson was nowhere to be seen.

"Where is he?" Roderic demanded.

"Where is who?" she asked, her voice testy with annoyance.

"Mr. Hugh B. Garson, of course."

"Mr. Garson?" she asked, all innocence. "I did observe Mrs. Jeanne Atkinson walking with him and two of his dogs in Hyde Park the other afternoon, so perhaps you will find him in Somers Town. Other than that possibility, I have not the vaguest notion where Mr. Garson might be. Nor do I care."

He stared at her, not comprehending. Suddenly the truth burst upon him and he muttered an oath under his breath.

"Admit it," he said, "this was all a ploy of yours, a scheme, a deceitful charade meant to trick me into believing you and Mr. Garson not only meant to elope but were eloping. As if I ever could believe such a thing since I realize you possess more than a modicum of sense. Hugh B. Garson indeed! Nevertheless, I confess myself annoyed you could bring yourself to attempt even such a pale imitation of one of my own stratagems."

"A pale imitation, my lord?" she asked. "I think not! I do believe my ploy was a success while yours, as we both know, very often were not."

How extraordinary, he reflected, at the same time he had vowed to be more forthright with her she had seen fit to practice a deception on him. Even now he could scarcely believe she'd done it. Evidently they were more alike than he had ever imagined. Not that he was sorry: too much honesty could be fatal. But that she had compromised hers to lure him to London he found absolutely astounding.

While she had become a bit devious for his sake, he

had promised himself to become less so for hers. He wondered if all men and women who loved one another grew more alike with the passage of time.

He climbed into the carriage, avoiding the wolfhound on the floor, and sat beside her. "All this deception on your part was totally unnecessary," he said, "inasmuch as I intended to offer for you the moment you stepped off the ship in Marien-Holstein. Lothar will vouch for the truth of what I say."

He raised her hand to his lips. "Will you marry me, Celeste? I love you, I suppose I have since first I met you. I know I always will."

"Oh, yes," she said. "Yes, yes, yes."

"Rather than return to town, shall we go on?" he asked. "To Gretna Green?"

She nodded. "Be warned," she said, "the road may be rough in places, the way uncertain." He realized she referred not so much to the road to the north but to their future together.

"I have no fears," he said. "Do you?"

She shook her head as she murmured, "None at all. Why should I? I love you and for me that's quite enough."

Taking her into his arms, he kissed her tenderly and, as always, lost himself in the wonder of her, the kiss deepening until he was swept up in an urgent tide of passion.

Gretna Green, he reminded himself, was miles and miles away. If only he could invent an excuse to pause on the way, to stop at a country inn where he could be alone with her. Perhaps he could suggest that the dogs needed a run. No, damn it, then he might well be forced to walk them.

Celeste drew away. "The wheel," she said.

"The wheel?" he echoed even as his lips again sought hers.

"The carriage wheel." She turned her face aside. "Before you overtook us," she told him, "I noticed a jarring coming from the rear wheel on the right side, a slight but disturbing wobbling."

"Obviously that wheel should be repaired before we suffer an accident."

"We could stop and have it seen to," she said. "Perhaps at the next country inn."

He stared at her. "I quite agree," he said, smiling.

His smile quickly changed to a laugh. How delightful she was, how full of surprises. The road ahead of them, he decided, might very well be rough at times—but it would never, ever be boring.